Eric

Be good to Jesu

The BLOODY SEVENS

Charles E. Hayes

(MSgt, USAF, Retired)

Edited by LTC Rick McClure

U.S. Army (Retired)

D1712943

ISBN-13: 978-1500471293
ISBN-10: 1500471291

DEDICATION

My family

A settler at the stockade wall

CONTENTS

ACKNOWLEDGMENTS

H. David Wright for use of his art on the cover and Graphic Enterprises for use of their photographs.   The authors Janice Holt Giles and Jesse Stuart for modeling to me that a Kentucky Mountain boy could write. To **LTC Rick McClure, U.S. Army (Ret)** for editing the manuscript.

2008 C. Hayes

Prologue

Kentucky!

Kentucky. The very word seemed to taste good in your mouth when you said it. Kentucky. A place that was fresh and pure. A place that was not yet tainted by laws and the British influence. A place that the British did not want us to go since they had signed the proclamation of 1763 forbidding us to settle in Kentucky.

The Hell with King George, Kentucky was where we would live. Kentucky is where our children will play and grow up.

Kentucky is the land of promise toward which the boldest men with the wildest spirits in the colonies have been waiting for. Recently received letters from settlers in Kentucky told that New-Year's Day of 1777, despite a heavy snow-fall and extreme cold, was celebrated in this wilderness by hundreds of settlers at the forts in Harrodsburg, Boonesborough, and St. Asaphs. The celebration and merrymaking of this New-Year's Day seemed to promise the settlers that the goals and promises of Kentucky were being fulfilled.

But, like I said, King George III didn't want American settlers in Kentucky. No sir, King George did not want us anywhere near Kentucky. King George is a damn fool.

Anywhere that King George didn't want me to be was a place I was going to go just out of plain cussedness. I hadn't had anything to do with King George and little to do with the British. Furthermore, I didn't want anything to do with them.

If anybody had asked me what I was doing going to Kentucky with Jacob, I'd have just told them, "A man has to be somewhere doing something."

Now, I had helped stop them from taking Charles Town, South Carolina, in 1776. Ten of us had signed up to join the militia. When the militia said we couldn't go to Charles Town to fight the British, we went anyway. There was a lot of shooting of cannons and a lot of British ships trying to knock out a palmetto and dirt fort so they could turn their cannons on Charles Town but they British ships couldn't knock down the fort to get close enough to Charles Town to do any damage.

The British had arrived in Cape Fear in March. They had figured on getting a passel of Tory support, but they were in for a surprise. We had whipped their Tory support in February at the Battle of Moore's Creek Bridge. British navy ships with Parker and Cornwallis only started arriving in late April and it was late May before all the ships got there.

The British navy didn't get pass the palmetto fort.

But now it was 1777 and I was entering Kentucky. Kentuck-key, a place that promised success and struggle, adventure and adversity. I couldn't help walking faster through Cumberland Gap to enter the promised land of Kentucky.

Kentucky had been home to Indians for untold hundreds of years until the late 1600's. The last Indian town had been abandoned in Kentucky about twenty years before I got there.

Now, in early 1777, there were no permanent Indian settlements or towns in Kentucky. All this was just fine with me. I wasn't really partial to Indians anyway.

From what I had been told by folks who traded with the Cherokee, there were a lot of Indians living in Kentucky about a hundred years ago. These Indians were from many different tribes. No one knew how many tribes. No one knew why they left. There was some talk that the Iroquois had claimed Kentucky and had run the others off. Right now, the Cherokee and Shawnee both hunted in Kentucky.

By rights, the Indians had no claim to Kentucky. The Iroquois had sold put to the British in 1768. The Shawnee and their allies had sold out at the end of Lord Dunmore's War and the Cherokee had sold their part of Kentucky to Judge Richard Henderson at Sycamore Shoals barely two years before.

I knew that Doctor Thomas Walker had scouted out part of Kentucky and had gone so far as to name Cumberland Gap in honor of the Duke of Cumberland, whoever the hell he was. Walker hadn't been real impressed by what he saw of Kentucky but I allowed that he was probably wrong.

There was one concern about the Cherokee sale. A renegade Cherokee known as Dragging Canoe was against it and he had a following.

After the Treaty of Sycamore Shoals, there had been a passel of folks going to Kentucky. This stream of settlers was slowed considerable after the British commenced to paying the Shawnee to attack American settlers. When I entered Kentucky with Jacob Hensley and ten others, there were probably less than three hundred white Americans in the whole of Kentucky.

I aimed to make a go of it in Kentucky. I willed myself to succeed. Just as sure as my name was Hugh Mason, I would succeed in Kentucky or I would die trying.

Kentucky, where our children would play and grow up.

1

KENTUCKY BOUND

(APRIL 1777)

My name is Hugh Mason. I can still remember the first time when I stretched out and breathed deeply of the forest scented air of Kentucky. I would have sworn, if anyone had bothered to ask, that the air was fresher and better in Kentucky than in Carolina. I was like a little young'un. I almost shook with excitement but I hid this from Jacob Hensley, the leader, and the other ten men in the party. It wouldn't do to have them think that I was out of control and could not be counted on to do my part.

I was pretty content to just lean back against an oak and stretch for a while. We had been moving since daybreak and I was enjoying the chance to rest up a bit while the noon sun was high. I also enjoyed listening to Jacob.

Jacob Hensley had hunted west of the mountains, part of that time in Kentucky, for over ten winters. His first winter's work had been stolen by the Cherokee and the second by the Shawnee. That was when he figured out that they had been keeping tabs on him and waited until he had his deerskins baled and ready to take back to the settlements before they robbed him. He had just finished retelling this to some of the party. Jacob was talking mostly to Carl. I couldn't tell whether he was wasting his wisdom on Carl or not. Carl usually couldn't tell the difference between somebody yarning him or telling him the gospel truth. The worst part of it was that If Carl had to guess between the two, like as not he'd get it wrong.

"You got to watch out for Injuns, they can be real sneaky," Jacob said as a conclusion to his tale."

Carl showed his doubt. "Jacob, why do you reckon they didn't kill you?"

Jacob turned to Carl, who was clearly unconvinced, and told him, "They didn't kill me because they wanted me to come back and kill more deer so I could gather up another pile of deerskins for them to steal."

Carl's expression plainly showed his continued disbelief. While Carl didn't believe Jacob, he didn't know how to express this disbelief without calling Jacob a liar. Jacob gave him an out.

"Carl, I'm sure that they wanted to steal more from me. Injuns don't think like we do. I heard one tale about longhunters who had a hunting camp in the Powell Valley. According to the tale I heard, they set up a camp about twelve maybe fifteen miles south, southwest of where Martin's Station is now. It is a very rich piece of land that is now called the Rob Camp. There stands, if you look real close, what is left of an old hunting camp. Around 1770, three fully equipped man with six horses built a hunting camp there. They had a good set up. They hunted all during the fall, winter and way deep into the spring of the year. Now these longhunters did their best to get along with the Injuns. The Injuns visited their camp pretty regular and bragged on what good hunters they were and all. The hunters tried to learn the Injun's talk and customs. Pretty soon, they could carry on talk without having to sign much. These experienced hunters allowed as they had lifelong friends in these worthless lying savages, which kind of tells me they were not the sharpest axes at the woodpile. You see, they didn't know just how different Injuns are from us. With what I know today, you will never catch me getting that close to Injuns. Well these hunters were all packed up and ready to leave. A whole a passel of the Injuns they thought were their friends showed up. The Injuns surrounded them and forced them to give them all their furs, skins, equipment, guns and horses. They told them it was a trade. They gave the hunters two broken muskets, two old plow horses and a pouch of rocks. They also told the hunters that if they ever returned, they would be killed."

While Carl stared, Jacob continued, "You see, the Injuns think this is all a big joke. They do not think stealing from us is wrong. It's all just a big joke."

"A big joke?"

"Yep, a big joke."

"But I thought that the Injuns attacked us because they wanted to run us off their land."

"Not likely, well, some maybe but most of the attacks by the Injuns come from them being hired by the Frenchies to attack the British towns and people." Jacob paused, then continued, "The British done the same thing with their Injuns. Hired 'em to attack the French and the French Injuns. Why I been told that the French priests told their Injuns that the British was the ones who crucified Jesus."

"Why that's a damn lie!"

"Of course it's a damn lie, not that I wouldn't put it past King George and his parliament to do something like that."

"Now Jacob, I done told you, I aint all that agin the king. I figure that if those folks up in Boston hadn't stirred things up, that we would be all right."

"Carl, you may be a little bit right, but not much. You see, I figure when all the high-toned British officers come over here with Braddock and Amherst and all that bunch; that they saw how big and rich and wonderful this place is and they didn't want us to spread out over too much of it."

"How do you figure that?"

"Why back in 1763, King George signed a proclamation forbidding anyone to settle where we are sitting right now."

"Why would he do that?"

"Carl, I've been told that a man can ride across any country in the old world in no time at all ---- less than a month easy with a middling horse and sometimes in less time. How long do you reckon it would take to get from the Atlantic Ocean to Cumberland Gap?"

"I don't know, I never seen the ocean."

"How long from Charles Town, South Carolina to Boston?"

"I don't know, I never been to either of those places either."

"It would take a sight longer."

"I reckon it would but I still don't see what you are getting at."

"What I'm getting at is that we are only good for the kings and such over there as long as they can control us. Most of the fancy-coated British officers that came over to fight the French has kinfolk that are high tooting men. When they were told just how big this country is and how free thinking we are, they knowed right off that they had to grab control in a hurry. They weren't slick enough to grab that control."

"But weren't we all British before that Boston bunch got everything all stirred up?"

"No, there are folks here who came from Holland, Germany and some other countries too. We come from people from places besides England. My ma told me her folks were close kin to folks back in Sweden --- wherever that is. Ma claimed we used to be Vikings and were a seafaring bunch. I don't reckon she had any call to lie to me."

"No Jacob, Carl was quick to agree, "I don't reckon your ma would lie to you, but how did all those folks get over here?"

"Most came as indentured servants. Some still come as indentured servants I guess. Of course we get a lot of slaves from Africa too. Some of the colonies were started to make a few people rich --- maybe all of them were --- I don't know."

"A man named James Oglethorpe and some of his friends got up a plan to settle Georgia. It is said that he wanted to send poor people to where they had a chance to have a better life. In England, a man could be hung for stealing a loaf of bread and a lot of people sure needed someplace to go. Georgia was named for King George II and some folks contributed money to help the poor who were sent to Georgia get started. William Penn founded Pennsylvania. He was a rich man and the King owed his pa a pile of money. The King of England figured it was cheaper to give William Penn a passel of land instead of money. William Penn allowed Quakers to settle in Pennsylvania no matter where they came from."

Jacob paused for a drink of water before continuing, "I reckon Massachusetts was started by puritans who settled the

Plymouth Colony and another bunch of them who started the Massachusetts Bay Colony. "

While they were talking, I was beginning to feel uneasy. I looked and listened but didn't hear anything except us and our horses. I stopped paying so much attention to Jacob listened to the forest. I stopped Jacob's talking by waving my left hand. Jacob stopped talking and whispered, "What is it?"

"I don't know," I told him, "Something doesn't feel exactly right."

It was true. I didn't know. I could not for the life of me explain why I felt this way. I had been a hunter and woodsman since I first went with his pa, more than ten years before. I had a feeling for the way the woods were supposed to feel and learned to know when the feeling was different.

Jacob didn't question me any further. He took his rifle and pouch with powderhorn attached and moved quietly behind the cover of another oak. Nine of the remaining ten men did likewise. None of the twelve of us showed any visible sense of alarm or urgency. The tenth man, Matt Walden was already sheltered beneath the shade of some laurel bushes and was probably sleeping. No one thought to wake him. Hugh shifted his knife and belt ax into convenient reach and listened to the forest.

We were under no illusion that we were well hidden. We were in a small grove surrounded by a few yards of ground too rocky and traveled over for forest growth to accumulate. We were around our saddle and pack horses which were never completely silent. Then too, we had stopped on or near the "Warriors Path."

For hundreds of years, Indians had traveled through the Cumberland Gap along a game trail known by the Shawnee as *Athiamiowee*, "the path of the armed ones." Rumors of a "Path of the Armed Ones," or the "Warrior's Path," which followed an ancient trail formed by flowing water from the slopes of the mountains had been told for years. It just took the longhunters a long time to find it. The path had been traveled for hundreds, possibly thousands of years. First by game and then by different tribes. The Indians traveled on the path for both trading and raiding. The path was a narrow, well-traveled trail.

That trail had various names; as the use of the path changed, the name changed to reflect that use. The Wasioto, The *Athiamiowee*, the Path of the Armed Ones, The Warrior's Path, and now part of it overlapped the Boone Trace. Thomas Walker, the first European who came down that path with his group, found the gap and recorded his observations. He named that section of the mountains the Cumberland Mountains after the Duke of Cumberland in England. The gap came to be called the Cumberland Gap.

We kept quiet and still. We waited. Close to or maybe even on the Warrior's Path, we waited, watched and listened. We knew real quick that we were not alone. The restlessness of our horses told us that. Jacob, me and all the others remained alert. None were sure of what the threat might be from. We finally decided the threat must be from renegade Cherokees that the Wataugans called Chickamauga.

The Chickamauga were members of the Cherokee who broke away after the treaty of Sycamore Shoals that sold Kentucky to the Transylvania Land Company. They were led by Dragging Canoe and were allied with the British. I had been told that during the previous winter of 1776/1777, they had moved down the Tennessee River to a more isolated area. There they established new towns to gain distance from the colonist. The Watauga settlers called Dragging Canoe and his band, with their new towns on the Chickamauga River, Chickamauga.

The high state of alertness and tension within the group was interrupted by the sound of snoring. Matt Walden always took an afternoon nap, when he could. When Matt Walden took a nap, he usually snored. The tension within then group increased but Jacob motioned for everyone to stay put.

Everyone did stay put but wondered what Jacob had on his mind. While they watched, Jacob loosened his camp ax and knife. He then pointed to every other man, except the sleeping Matt, and said, 'Don't fire at the first charge."

The men nodded and got ready for an attack. Matt just continued to sleep and to snore comfortably. The Indians must have been convinced by Matt's snoring that our group was simply resting. Whatever the reason, they charged into us.

They charged with fearsome shouts that none of us will ever forget. The screams could have confused an unaware group into panic and maybe inaction but Jacob had this group armed, alert and ready for an attack. Six of our men fired and four Indians dropped.

Three of the fallen were already dead. One fell with two fatal wounds and a fourth made a bloody trail as he retreated. A later shot from a trade musket dropped one of Jacob Hensley's party. The closeness of both sides turned the melee into a vicious hand to hand struggle. Knife and tomahawk against knife and camp ax. I countered a tomahawk blow with my rifle barrel and pushed my long knife into the attacker's vitals. I held my rifle tightly in my left hand.

It was immediately obvious that the Chickamauga out-numbered the Hensley party but the five unfired rifles turned the tables. Jacob had taught us to stay in a circle in order to have support when attacked. He also had us make up paper cartridges containing from eight to twelve .30 caliber balls. These paper cartridges were shaped to be ripped with your teeth to dump the powder down the muzzle and the rest of the cartridge dropped on top of the powder charge. This method wouldn't win any shooting matches but just might get us through a close fight like this one.

We stayed in our close circle and fought back the best we could. We hoped it would be good enough. When I got the chance, I fired and reached for a paper cartridge. Two others fired at the attackers and gave us a little breathing space to reload. While we reloaded, the two who had been too busy to fire made up for lost time. The continuing fire seemed to confuse the attackers. Three newly fallen attackers caused a pause in the fight. We used the time that to reload our weapons and fire a staggered volley.

Like I said, this reloading was not the typical reloading operation of a rifle. Instead of ramming a tight patched round ball onto a powder charge, an operation that might take from half a minute to a whole minute, shortcuts were taken. Each shooter ripped open a paper cartridge with his teeth, dumped the powder into the muzzle and dropped the remainder of the paper cartridge, which held eight to twelve round balls down the muzzle and sometimes rammed a pad of leather on top of the cartridge. The shooter then pulled the stopper from their powderhorn and primed the pan of their weapon. This operation took no more than ten to twenty seconds

As fast as my rifle was reloaded, I pointed it at an enemy and fired. Two more of our party dropped, wounded but we didn't know how badly. We not only held our own but our firing took six more of the attackers out of action. As the attackers regrouped to attack, a shrieking, squalling bedlam of noise came from the east of them. I was surprised by the caterwauling but figured it was probably either reinforcements for the Indians or a wildcat had bit its own tail and didn't know how to stop.

The Chickamauga stopped. They were more surprised and startled by the unfamiliar racket than we were. While the attackers hesitated before rushing forward, four of the defenders fired a volley of .30 buckshot into the mass of them. As the Chickamauga reeled, the rest of us fired a volley into the attacking Chickamauga. They hadn't aimed to but those Indians had charged into a wall of .30 caliber buck shot. The attackers were falling and the shrieking was getting nearer. Hugh and three others who had fired the first volley figured out who was the leader of the attackers and they all fired at him. Hit by over twenty .30 caliber balls, he fell like a stone.

In the confusion that followed, the remaining attackers fled.

Photo by Jim Cummings (2010) of graphicenterprises.net, pioneer times. Jim and Kathy Cummings have possibly the best re-enactment website in the cyber world.

2

Recovery

Within seconds, not a single attacking, living Chickamauga was in sight. A quick investigation showed that all the attackers who had fallen were either dead or dying. I helped Wayne and Wade Morris separate all the weapons from the hostiles and verified that the killed were actually dead. It was a known fact that Indians were good hands at playing 'possum. Jacob supervised the care of the four men from our party who had fallen. Two were killed and two were wounded. I fell in with the others and made sure we secured our site and posted guards. For some of us, this wasn't our first fight. It wasn't even our first Indian fight. Besides, keeping busy kept us from remembering just how close it had been. Don't let anyone tell you that you should get used to this kind of fracas and can get over it real quick.

While this was going on, the shrieking bedlam of noise came closer. Soon a small party led by a youth playing a bagpipe could be seen. As the group neared, they began cheering and broke into a run.

I just stopped what I was doing and stared. The rest of Jacob's party was as surprised as I was. They just stared in amazement. As the group arrived, they stopped in confusion.

"Where's Patrick?"

"What?"

"Where's Patrick?"

Jacob shrugged, "I don't know where Patrick is, in fact, I don't think I know Patrick."

The questioner, apparently the leader of the small party, stared at the remains of the recent battle and sat down. He paled and appeared both sweaty and cold. The sight of a grave being dug for the two slain members of our party and the Indian dead being dragged away unnerved him. The rest of his party gathered around him and spoke in low tones. Finally, their story began to be told.

"I'm Ronald Smith. We are part of a big group going to Kentucky. Patrick and five others were going on ahead of us to find a good camping place inside Kentucky. There's another, larger group, behind us. When Patrick saw us getting close, they were going to fire their guns and we were all going to celebrate being in Kentucky. We heard the shooting and thought you were Patrick so we started celebrating too."

"Might be a good thing for us that you did," commented Jacob, "those damn Injuns didn't know what was coming."

"Where's Patrick?"

Jacob shrugged, "I don't know. Let's go a little further and see if we can find him."

I didn't expect to find Patrick and those with him alive. Nor did anyone else in our party. We hoped to, but we didn't expect to, find him alive. We were right. Five miles further we run across an eastbound party that was burying Patrick and his comrades.

Jacob led our party to where a large grave was being dug. Ronald Smith looked at the scalped and mutilated bodies and retched. Jacob and the rest of us helped with the digging and the bodies were buried without being read over. There were several nearly silent prayers.

Jacob waited until the tasks were completed before asking questions. The eastbound party was scared and looked scared. They constantly peered into the darkening forests that surrounded them. After first posting sentries, Jacob asked the question that both he and the rest of us wanted to know the answer to, "Why are you leaving Kentucky and where did you come from?"

The man nearest Jacob answered, "First off, we come from Harrodsburg. We're leaving because the damn Injuns are too riled up for us to stay."

"What happened?"

"Everything was going fine. The winter had been pretty cold and we got more snow than we expected but it wasn't bad. There was still snow on the ground in March and we were sorting out seeds so we could plant our crops as soon as the weather allowed. It was about that time that scouts began to come in with reports of Injun sign. A lot of Injun sign but we hadn't seen any of them. All the folks in the fort went on with getting ready for planting and building up their places. Then one day a boy named Jim Ray comes come a running into the fort a hollering about Injuns."

The speaker paused long enough to drink some water. Lowering his noggin, he continued, "About four or five miles from the fort there was half-grown men working in a sugar maple grove.

Their names was Coomes, Shores and the two Ray brothers, Will and Jim. The boys were busy working and had seen no sign of any hostiles. Everything seemed real peaceable. There was no sign of any danger. They didn't have a chance. Without any warning, an Injun shot and killed Will Ray. The other three tried to escape. Coomes jumped into a bunch of brush and didn't leave any tracks so he was able to stay hid. Shores was caught and made a captive, we think. We never found his body so we reckon he was captured."

The speaker stopped talking and one of his companions took up the tale. "The fourth man, Jim Ray, could run like a bat trying to get out of Hell. Once he got started and got a going, nobody could catch him. I don't reckon any of the red dogs got close enough to shoot him. It wasn't much more than thirty minutes before he come running through the fort gates a hollering about Injuns. Now everybody was all tore up and no one was real sure what would be the best thing to do. Hugh McGary is the stepfather of Will Ray and he wanted to take a bunch of men and go to the rescue. Jim Harrod didn't think that would be a good idea. Jim thought the hostiles might want to bait a trap for any rescue party and then attack the weakened fort. They both had words and come near to shooting each other. They both raised their guns when Hugh McGary's wife pushed herself between the two men and grabbed her husband's rifle. Things calmed down and McGary gathered up thirty volunteers and they rode to the maple grove. When they reached the grove, they found the scalped and mutilated remains of Will Ray. They say that McGary went crazy. He wanted to go after the hostiles and kill them all. They found Coomes alive and rescued him. They didn't find any sign of Shores or any of the red devils that captured him."

After a pause, he continued, "I would not want to be any Injun that McGary runs into.[1] Things got worse a few days later

---

[1] When Hugh McGary found a Shawnee wearing his stepson's shirt, he killed the Shawnee and fed his body to his dogs.

when we saw a cabin outside the fort on fire. We tried to put out the fire but we got ambushed by a bunch of hostiles. We fought but they outnumbered us and we were real lucky to make it back into the fort. The Injuns set up a camp in sight of the fort. For days, they ignored us. They acted like they were all by themselves and that we weren't even there. Then, all of a sudden, they all charged the fort. They kind of took us by surprise but before they reached the walls, forty or fifty of us were at the walls and fired at them. We kept firing until they quit. It was pretty touchy for a while but we held them off. Then they left and after they left, we left."

At the end of his story, he looked at Jacob and the rest of the newcomers. Pointing to the new grave, he announced, "If you don't leave with us, right there is what your fate will be."

Carl turned to Jacob and asked, "Does this sound like the Injun sense of humor you were telling me about?"

"No, Carl, it sounds to me like they are being paid by the British to attack us."

"How do you figure that?"

Jacob walked over to the pack that had all the weapons salvaged from the Chickamauga attackers and began holding them up. As he showed them, he told the group, "New trade guns, new knives, new tomahawks; I didn't see an old blade or gun in the whole pack that attacked us. Just how do you figure that bunch of young bucks could have got armed like that if somebody hadn't armed them?"

"What do you mean?"

"Every one of the Indians we killed or saw, I'd say, were no more than seventeen or eighteen years old. Except for the leader. He looked to be a few years older. It's a lucky thing for us too. Older and more experienced men would have killed more of us, maybe would have wiped us out. They probably wanted our horses. Like as not, one of them jumped first and the others followed. The older man in charge didn't have a chance to get control and we got lucky killing him. Somebody paid for their new guns. Somebody paid for their new knives. Somebody paid for their new tomahawks. I'd say the money came from the British. I'd say the British are paying good money for all the trouble going on here in Kentucky right now."

I had to agree with Jacob. None of our horses had been touched and this attack wasn't like any I had ever experienced or heard about. As a general rule, Indians are real good at hiding, ambushing and murdering. It is hard for a white man to imagine the pains they go through to hide and protect themselves while murdering their enemies. They can hide in grass that you wouldn't think would hide a dog. They hide in thickets so good you can stare right at them and never see them. They can hide among or in trees, in a creek bed or about anywhere. They can stay still and quiet until their target gets within reach and then strike.

Like Jacob said, Indians have a strange sense of humor. I have heard of them waiting outside a cabin door just to kill the first person to open the door. If the Indian gets a chance, he'll take scalps. They needed the scalp to sell to the British.

Indians can sometimes cut off a station or fort from help. They will try to starve the people into surrendering or trying to escape. When it comes to tricking the settlers into a trap, they have no equal. If Indians attack from the north, somebody had damn sure better be watching the south. After they attack, they know that either scalps or captives can be sold to the British. Sometimes it is easier to kill half a dozen women and children that to take one captive.

The settlers who persevered and stayed in Kentucky learned to be careful. The bravery of these settlers who left a familiar life to risk such an enemy in the wilderness is nothing short of remarkable. It is utterly amazing and astonishing that so many settlers stayed in Kentucky instead of retreating east through Cumberland Gap.

Stay the settlers did. They stayed in Kentucky and they raised families and crops. They put up with forting up (living in forts) when they thought danger was coming and fought when they had to fight. Eventually, they took the fight to the enemy

The population of settlers in Kentucky increased to over a thousand in 1776. That population changed real quick after the non-stop Indian raids started. Many settlers fled east where it was safer. There were less than 300 settlers in Kentucky when we arrived. After the attacks of 1777, Kentucky's population started to grow and continued to grow.

I sure had to hand it to Jacob. Jacob was a thinking man and educated more than most. I had heard somewhere that Jacobs's pa had been a preacher who wrote letters to men throughout the colonies and even back in England, Ireland and Scotland. It was said that he had even wrote to and received letters from Benjamin Franklin. I knew for a fact that Jacob sent and received a lot of letters.

We all knew that staying in Kentucky would be dangerous. We knew that if they could, the Indians would kill us or drive us out back across the mountains. We also knew that the British were making it worth their while to attack us and generally pester us back east of the Mountains.

We knew it.

I knew it.

I didn't aim to go back to the east side of the mountains.

Carl and several others decided to return to the Yadkin Valley of North Carolina. I decided to stay with Jacob in Kentucky. The two Morris brothers, Wayne and Wade, decided to continue on into Kentucky with us.

The last thing Carl said to me was. "I don't see any reason for you to head into trouble in Kentucky."

Without a pause, I answered, "A man has to be somewhere doing something."

Jacob

3

JACOB

We left the eastbound crowd before daybreak. Jacob wanted us to get a good start before it got to be good light. We took the muskets we had salvaged from the fight along with most of the powder and lead balls. Travel was kind of slow in the dark but it was soon apparent that Jacob had been on this trace before. The sun was almost three hours high before we stopped to water ourselves and our horses.

I figured this would be a good time to talk to Jacob about our plans. I say our plans but at that point, I wasn't sure what they were. I waited until we had all drunk our fill and were together. I didn't aim to cause any hard feelings by leaving out Wayne and Wade.

"Jacob, where exactly are we heading to now? Fort Boones-borough?

Then Jacob surprised me, "I'm not sure. Maybe Boones-borough but I want to find out what is going on first. I don't want us to walk into a mess of Shawnee and British." "There is a fort at Harrodsburg and there are – or were – several stations. We need to find one that we can get in where we will have a chance at surviving."

"How are we going to decide?"

"I expect we will run into more people leaving Kentucky. We'll try to find out from them what is going on."

Like I said. Jacob was a smart man. He was probably a lot smarter than me but that don't take much. More to the point, Jacob had spent time in Kentucky and had a better idea of what we were up against.

Jacob was right. We ran into more people leaving Kentucky. We were almost to the Hazel Patch[2] when we ran into folks with news about Boonesborough. Boonesborough had been attacked shortly after the Shawnee had left Fort Harrod. These folks had left other stations and were on their way to Boonesborough when they got word that there were more Shawnee around Boones-borough than fleas on a dog. That encouraged them to return to Virginia for a while. We met them about midafternoon and they were of no mind to stay and talk. They strongly suggested we leave with them and then were on their way.

Jacob fell in back on the trace and we went with him. I could tell he was studying about the whole situation so I didn't bother him. We got to the spot on the trace known as the Hazel Patch and stopped. Jacob's eyes were closed and he was talking softly. I realized that he was praying.

Jacob opened his eyes, raised his head, straightened and told us, "We are following Skaggs' Trace to the west."

Skaggs Trace was named after Henry Skaggs. He was a hunter, explorer and pioneer. He hunted over and explored the

---

[2] Early journal entries referred to "the Hazel Patch" and "the Crab Orchard." Later interviews by John Dabney Shane referred to these locations in this manner. The author elects to use this method as opposed to Hazel Patch and Crab Orchard.

frontiers of Tennessee and Kentucky from 1761until now. He began as a longhunter. Later, he worked with Daniel Boone for Judge Richard Henderson.

In 1761, Skaggs joined an expedition led by Elisha Walden into Carter's Valley in Tennessee. Two years later he explored the Cumberland Mountains and valleys more thoroughly. In 1764, Skaggs led his first crew through Cumberland Gap. News of these jaunts reached Daniel Boone. Boone is said to have talked Judge Richard Henderson into hiring Skaggs to help Boone as an agent of Henderson's land company. During 1765, Skaggs explored the lower Cumberland River and established his station there. Skaggs Trace begins at the Hazel Patch and continues west as far as the Crab Orchard.

The twenty years before Henderson bought Kentucky from the Cherokee at the Treaty of Sycamore Shoals, longhunters hunted and explored Kentucky and other lands west of the mountains. Elisha Walden hunted through Powell's Valley. There, he found an Indian trail that led his party through the Cumberland Gap and into Kentucky. Elisha Walden and his party explored the Cumberland River Valley and country side until they reached Laurel Mountain. The presence of Indians at Laurel Mountain made them decide to return to east of the Cumberland Gap. In the party with Walden were Henry Skaggs, William Blevins, Charles Cox, and fifteen to twenty longhunters. Their presence is shown by Walden's Mountain, Walden's Creek, Skaggs' Ridge and Newman's Ridge, which they named.

In 1766, James Smith, Joshua Horton, Uriah Stone, William Baker, and a young slave entered Kentucky through the Cumber-land Gap. They hunted in the Cherokee country along the Cumberland and Tennessee rivers. Isaac Lindsey led another party from South Carolina into Kentucky as far as a tributary of the Cumberland which they named Stone's River. There on Stone's River, they met Jim Harrod and Michael Stoner. Harrod and Stoner had come into Kentucky using the Ohio River from Fort Pitt. Other longhunters like Daniel Boone and Casper Mansker knew a right smart about Kentucky. By the time Judge Richard Henderson sealed his deal with the Cherokee, A lot of longhunters knew a lot about Kentucky. I found out that one of the most experienced longhunters was Jacob Hensley.

We set out right then, west on Skaggs Trace. It was at the Hazel Patch that I began to suspect that Jacob knew more about Kentucky than he had mentioned. Skaggs Trace was plainly marked but Jacob left the trace and by evening we were camped beside a spring of cold, fresh water that was four or five miles from the trace. This happened every evening. It didn't take a schoolteacher to see that Jacob knew what he was doing.

Jacob pushed us hard. He said that if we were caught that we were as good as dead. We moved fast but we moved on rested horses. That is a pretty good way to move but it's easier to say it than to do it.

While we traveled, I began to try to size Jacob up. Out here, in wild country and away from neighbors and churches and little villages, Jacob appeared different. Except for the times he was on a long hunt or I was, I had known Jacob most of my life. He was some different from most people but I just took that to be the way Jacob was.

Jacob was a longhunter but a lot of people sought him out to get his opinion on a whole passel of things. I remembered that a lawyer had spent a lot of time with Jacob before he tried a big case. I knew that before we left for Kentucky, Jacob had crated up a lot of books and left them with a storekeeper so he could send for them later. Most of the people I knew were lucky if the family had one book and that was usually the Bible.

Jacob received a lot of letters. He got letters from at least two people in each of the British colonies and some from England, Scotland and Ireland. I later found that he tried to get the views of people on different sides of an argument. That way he had a better handle on what the truth of something was.

I had never read any of the letters. The truth is, back then I couldn't read much at all. I could read some but when you don't have anything to read, it's easy to get out of the habit. Not that I had ever been in the habit of reading but I had three years of schooling. Come to think of it, Jacob was my teacher part of that time.

Don't get me wrong. My family was good people. They just weren't as strong on reading and schooling as Jacob. My family was more about hard work from can-see until can't-see. Most of the folks I knew were like that.

Now that I thought about it, Jacob had a family once. He had a wife who died during childbirth. Seemed I remembered that the baby lived and had been sent to Jacob's sister in Tarboro or somewhere. I remembered my ma a saying that it was best to have a woman raise a little girl.

One night, I asked Jacob, "Do you have any books with you?"

Jacob straightened like he had heard a timber rattler shaking its beads. "Yes, I've got three."

"How come you don't read them on the trail or in camp?"

"Out here, a man had best not get distracted by anything. A distracted man or a man not paying attention to what's going on around him can be a dead man in a hurry."

"Is reading that much trouble? I'd never thought of it as distracting to a body."

"Hugh, when a man reads, he has to apply everything he already knows to what he is reading. He's got to take it apart and put it back together and make sure it's right."

Now I was confused. "But it's all writ down. Don't that make it right?"

"No. It may be what someone thinks is the truth, it might be what he wants you to think the truth is, but it isn't necessarily the truth."

That I did not understand. I could not understand why someone would go to the trouble to write something down if it wasn't the truth. That is what I told Jacob.

Jacob took the time to listen to the night noises and check the horses before he answered.

"Hugh, if you read that declaring independence from England was the smartest thing done in ten years, what would you say?"

"Why I'd say that's right. That's the kind of things that should be wrote."

"Suppose you read that declaring independence from England was the stupidest thing done in ten years, what would you say?"

"Why, I guess I'd say that it was a damn lie."

"Yes! But both thoughts were written down. If one is right then the other must be wrong."

"Then how does a man know which is right and which is wrong."

"That, Hugh, is why I don't read when I am traveling through country where there's apt to be Indians. That's also why I prefer to have talks like this when there are four walls of safety around us."

I just nodded and commenced to checking the forest around us.

Everything sounded good and I figured we were safe but I hunkered down and rested quietly. I figured that when we got to where we were going that I'd bring this reading thing up to Jacob again. Right then, I couldn't figure out whether it would be answers or confusion.

Being mindful of what Jacob had said, I began to check the forest around us again.

Photo by Jim Cummings graphicenterprises.net

4

LOGAN'S FORT

(MAY 1777)

I could tell that Jacob was a little surprised when we heard the sound of axes chopping. We had been traveling since long before daybreak and hadn't expected to find settlers this far from either Fort Harrod or Fort Boonesborough.

The four of us rode out of the forest and into a large clearing where a fort was almost constructed and getting the final touches. Jacob rode in first, waving his rifle in the air to attract attention. He needn't have done it for it was plain that they all saw us. A strong looking man who appeared to be in his middle thirties walked toward Jacob with a big grin. I didn't know who he was until Jacob spoke.

"Ben Logan, what have you got out here?"

Benjamin Logan entered to the country in 1775. He came to make a good life for himself and his family. I don't think he moved to Kentucky to try to be a big wheel like a lot of people did. I think he moved to Kentucky to make a good life for himself and his family.

While I never asked, I always thought his parents came from Ireland as indentured servants. That was the way most people came to America. Just meeting him, I figured right off that he would be a leader before he was through. I was right.

Ben's father died when he was barely a man, just fifteen or sixteen years old. He then became the provider for his widowed mother and his younger brothers and sisters. By all accounts, he did a good job. He was a hard worker and a knowing man but he got very little education.

As far as education goes, it wasn't real plentiful. Three of the leaders of early Kentucky were Boone, Harrod, and Logan. I'd be hard pressed to say which one had the least school education[3]. Of course, all three had more common sense and common skills than a schoolhouse could hold and that is what Kentucky needed then.

I'd have to say that Ben Logan, above all else, was a good man. He was a good Christian and he had a good dose of common sense. Maybe that's all a man really needs.

I found out later that, as the eldest son, he could have taken all his father's holdings. He didn't. The story is that he insisted they be divided up among all his brothers and sisters with each getting

---

[3] Boone, Logan and Harrod could read and write. They probably received more teaching at home than in a school.

a share equal to his share.

Ben Logan, at the age of twenty-one, had accompanied Colonel Henry Louis Bouquet at the end of the French and Indian War and to help put down Pontiac's rebellion. The folks in charge of Ben noticed that he was a good leader and made him a sergeant. After mustering out of the army, Ben made sure his mother, brothers and sisters were settled comfortable and moved south to the Holston. He settled down there and married Ann.

Ben was a lieutenant in Lord Dunmore's war and was at the Battle of Point Pleasant. During the campaign, being a knowing man, he listened to men who had traveled west of the mountains and had a good look at what was there. I think he decided right then and there to make a move to the new lands.

He set his affairs in order, gave his mother everything he didn't need and set off for Kentucky. He met Daniel Boone in Powell's Valley and stayed with him as Boone blazed his trace as far north as the Hazel Patch.

At the Hazel Patch Logan, having talked with others who had been in Kentucky and grown a little doubtful about the future of Transylvania Company, left Boone and headed west on Skaggs Trace toward the Crab Orchard.

Logan found a likely spot and began to make his own place. That winter, he went back east and collected his family and moved them to their new home. Logan brought his family, a slave named Molly and her three sons, Matt, Dave, and Isaac. On the way back to Kentucky they were joined by Benjamin and Rebecca Pettit and their family.

By late summer or early fall, Indian trouble began. Being a thoughtful and knowing man, Logan began talking to settlers around Crab Orchard and let them know that they could join him for protection.

The people decided instead to flee to Fort Harrod and seek protection there. Some of these people were the same ones we met leaving Kentucky as we entered.

Logan, finding himself alone and an easy target, moved to Fort Harrod. Moving was a hard thing to do because it felt like giving up. It felt like quitting and Ben Logan was not a quitter. It was the right thing to do but Ben Logan was damn sure it was a temporary thing.

While at the fort, he found half a dozen families who were tired of forting up and persuaded them to return to his station with him. They were building a fort as we rode up.

Now we had been traveling steady and sleeping light. That made no difference. We got off our horses. We unsaddled and unpacked the horses, then wiped them down and tied them where there was grass and water.

We put our gear up, grabbed axes and began to help with the fort. I don't recall anybody asking or telling us what to do and I know I didn't ask what needed to be done. We just joined in and did it.

Benjamin Logan's Fort or Station was set on a slight height about fifty yards west of the smaller spring at St. Asaph. The fort was built of logs and was about 150 feet by 90 feet with blockhouses at three corners that rose higher than the walls of the fort and extended beyond the walls. This allowed the defenders to fire at any attacker who managed to get next to the walls and below the firing ports. There was a single cabin at the fourth corner. Gates were located at each end and were raised and lowered by leather ropes. The main gate faced east. Three cabins each formed the north and south walls, which were occupied by William Menniffee, William Whitley and the James Mason families. There were four cabins adjoining occupied by George Clark, Benjamin Logan, Benjamin Pettit and Samuel Coburn.

The fort's water came from a spring that lay roughly 50 yards to the east. A tunnel was dug from inside the southeastern block-house to the springhouse, which covered the spring. The tunnel was four feet deep and three feet wide. This was a thoughtful arrangement that allowed the settlers to get water without being seen if the fort was under siege by Indians. The land around the fort had been cleared of all trees and plants big enough to be used as cover. The work to remove the available cover was done to stop the Indians from having any cover to sneak close to the fort. The ridge to the south of St. Asaph's Branch was not yet completely cleared and most of the firing of Indian guns came from here. The distance between the fort and cover was 200 to 250 yards. This distance was too far for most Indian guns and far too great for arrows to have any effect. The care in building the fort and defending the fort was such that the fort did not fall despite being attacked by far superior numbers of attackers than there were defenders.

This working together, as we immediately began to do, was not unusual on the Kentucky Frontier. I aint saying that everybody did because anywhere you go, there are a few trifling folks. They are usually the first to go back or otherwise leave. The summer before, when there weren't many settlers, both Logan and Pettit wanted to improve their places and put in crops. It was too risky for one family to do this on their own so Logan and Pettit swapped work. For a week, the Logan's would stay with the Pettit's and Logan, with the slave boys Dave and Matt, would work on Pettit's place and crops. The following week, The Pettit's would stay and work at Logan's place.

Fortunately for Logan, Pettit had lived among and traded with the Indians. He was the one who began spotting Indian sign and talked Logan to going to Fort Harrod for protection. The two families stayed the winter of 1776/1777 in Fort Harrod. There, they met the Whitley, Clark and Menifee families. With three other families, they left Fort Harrod and returned to make Logan's Station defensible.

Logan build his station or fort for defense[4] and not for pretty. The fort (or station) was small enough to be defended by the small number of people who built it. There was a fine line between having a fort with enough room and a fort that could be defended. This fort was a fort that could be defended.[5] There was a cabin in the fort for each of the families who built the fort. It covered less than a half an acre. It was a hard day's journey from Fort Boonesborough and two day's hard journey from Fort Harrod.

By the time we arrived, during the spring of 1777, the Logans, Pettits, Whitleys, Menifees, Clarks, Masons and Coburns were busy building homes, lives and protection. Jacob, Wade, Wayne and I stayed in a blockhouse with the unmarried men and male slaves.

We were all busy getting ready for the Indian trouble we all expected to happen soon. We didn't have to wait long. Like Jacob had told us, the British were arming the Indians and urging them to attack American settlers. We later learned that the British were paying for captives and scalps.

The British commander in Detroit, General Henry Hamilton was called "the hair buyer" or "Hair Buyer" Hamilton because of his role in the "scalp buying trade." Hamilton bought all scalps. Scalps taken from men, women and children. The hypocrisy of the British made them voice the concern that only men of fighting age be murdered and scalped but they paid for all scalps.

At the time we got to Logan's Fort, there were no more than 150 men of fighting age in Kentucky. There were no more than 45 families in the whole of Kentucky. At Logan's Fort, there were only

---

[4] The Indians later referred to Logan's Fort as 'Standing Fort' because they could not capture it, despite its small size and number of defenders.

[5] The town that developed there was later called Stanford, some say derived from "Standing Fort.

19 men who could bear arms, counting us.

Women were a big help on the Kentucky Frontier. Some of the women could clean and reload rifles, fowlers and muskets. They could knap (sharpen) flints and mold bullets. Some of the women, like Esther Whitley and Jane Menifee were damn fine shots. Neither Esther nor Jane had any hesitation about drawing a bead on a hostile Indian. They were good at reloading and squeezing the trigger.

The women were also very valuable when it came to treating the sick and injured. Of course, Benjamin Pettit helped them. Ben knew folk and Indian methods of treating wounds and healing the sick. He had lived and traded amongst the Cherokee and even spoke some of their language. Ben helped, but the women did most of the doctoring and nursing.

Men and women, the forts and stations in Kentucky were filled with strong willed people with strong minds and strong ideas. Of course, having so many strong people was usually a good thing – but not all the time. Everyone acknowledged that Ben Logan was the leader[6] but he was not the only man there capable of leading or of being a good leader. Billy Whitley could have done the job.[7] So

---

[6] *Benjamin Logan became a colonel in the militia, he was second-in-command of all the militia in Kentucky. He was also to be a leader in Kentucky's efforts to become a state.*

[7] *Billy Whitley made it his personal mission to protect settlers on the Boone Trace. When depredations by the Chickamauga got beyond tolerable, he let militia into what is now Tennessee to attack the Chickamauga towns. Whitley knew that there was a strong British push behind the attacks. William Whitley hated the British. He hated the British so much that when he built a race course, he deliberately raced horses opposite the direction raced in England.*

could have Ben Pettit. Jacob or most of the other men could have been the leader.

The men weren't the only strong people there. The women were strong and capable as well. I don't recollect a single one of those women *swooning* or losing their head when the going got tough.

When women and children came to Kentucky, everything changed. Men by themselves didn't mind living in a quick built hut barely big enough to lie down in and only high enough to stand up in at the highest spot. With women and children to care for and protect, the men's habits and standards changed. They began building more permanent cabins. Some of these cabins had wooden floors right away and the rest had them real soon.

Women and children brought a sense of permanence and purpose to Kentucky. Without women and children, a man could pick up his gun and gear and leave for somewhere else. It was a sight more trouble to move a family.

Women and children meant gardens were planted and milk cows were necessary. Crops got tended and food put away for the winter. Some folks even brought in pigs, notched their ears and let them run loose in the woods.

Women and children also brought about the need for stronger forts and stations. With Indian trouble, women and children had to be in a fort and the men had to be with them. This meant the men could not hit the woods any time there was trouble. Everyone had to fort up.

The problem of forting up was that so many of the people were strong. While forting up, they had to live close to other strong people. This required that the strong people get along together. It wasn't as easy as it might sound. Some folks, Hugh McGary for example, never managed it.

When living close and surrounded by a hostile enemy that wanted to sell your scalps to the British, strong people had to get along and pay attention to the job of staying alive. Even with each family having their own cabin, folks lived real close. Folks could and did get on each other's nerves. Sometimes, it was a miracle that all the folks in a fort didn't kill each other before the Indians had a chance to kill them.

Logan's Fort was lucky in that each family had their own cabin. In some forts, there might be two or three families in each cabin. Of course having two or three families in each cabin would have meant more defenders inside the fort.

At this time, in 1777, Kentucky had three forts. These forts; Fort Harrod, Fort Boonesborough, and Logan's Fort were all that were left manned and defended. There had been others, like McClelland's Station, but the savage attacks of the previous summer and fall had caused many settlers to rethink staying in Kentucky. The population of settlers in Kentucky dropped in a matter of months from over a thousand to roughly two hundred.

The people at Logan's Fort aimed to stay. They were planting crops and tending them. They were clearing more land. We did note that we needed to clear away more of the cane that was close to the fort.

While preparing for the future, the folks were preparing for the short term. Water was hauled to the fort and stored. Food was dried and put away for emergency use. The extra weapons that Jacob had us collect from the Chickamauga were all cleaned and stored away where they would be handy.

Now these Indian trade guns weren't much, but they could come in handy. These guns were .60 caliber smooth bore, short and cheaply made. For any range over fifty yards (some would say thirty yards) they didn't come close to a rifles accuracy. On the plus side, though, they could be loaded quicker with buckshot or just about anything else. When it came to stopping a charge on a fort, those little Indian trade guns could spit out a lot of lead in a hurry.

Jacob had us manufacture paper cartridges for the trade guns. I guess he figured that if the sun was low and we weren't sleeping, we could make cartridges. Using the gunpowder we got from the killed Chickamauga, we made over one hundred cartridges.

The women helped us with this task. Jacob gave them the .60 caliber balls we took from the Chickamauga and they molded .30 caliber balls for us to place in the paper cartridges. After making the paper cartridges, Jacob stored them in a water tight wooden box. As things turned out, it was a damn good thing we made those cartridges.

Logan's Fort was a rectangle covering just under half an acre. The upright poles that formed part of the outer walls were set in a trench and forced close together. The part of the wall they formed was just a shade over ten feet high. We figured the walls would stand anything the Indians could throw at them. We could hold off the British too, unless the British brought cannon. The block houses or bastions, built at three of the four corners, extended over the lower story about eighteen inches so that no enemy could get beneath our fire by getting close to the wall.

The cabins in the fort formed part of the outer walls. The walls of the cabin that formed part of the defense were twelve to fourteen feet high and sloped steeply inward. This steepness was necessary in case fire arrows were shot on to the roof. The steepness made it easier for one of the boys to kick the arrows off the roof. The cabins had clapboard roofs, slab doors hung with leather hinges and windows covered with oiled paper. All of the cabins opened into the center of the fort.

The cabins were roughly fifteen by ten feet and consisted of one room with a sleeping loft for the children. These cabins were built quick to provide shelter and not meant to be permanent. The still crude but better and longer lasting cabins would happen later. The permanent houses came later still, like the fine house Billy Whitley built near the Crab Orchard. All Kentucky Pioneers knew that safety and survival came before ease and comfort. Later cabins and homes could be built for the long haul but surviving was the first thing on our list. I have got to say though, that the cabins and forts were built a whole lot better than they would have been if the women and children weren't in Kentucky with us. It seemed that men were more anxious to have wood floors and stone chimneys when there was a woman in the cabin.

One of the things that was high on our list was chinking or filling in the spaces of the cabin walls that formed part of the fort wall. No one wanted to leave a space between the logs that an Indian could sneak up, maybe at night, and fire into.

It could be said that we built the best we could with the time and the tools that we had. The time was stolen from the time we spent hunting, planting and watching for Indians. The tools were primarily axes. Each tool we used had been brought from east of the mountains and there weren't many.

Still, we did the best we could with what we had. It might not have been pretty but it was useful.

Whitley House near Crab Orchard, Kentucky as completed in 1794. It was the first brick house built in Kentucky. Photo by Jim Cummings (2010) of graphicenterprises.net, pioneer times. Jim and Kathy Cummings have possibly the best re-enactment website in the cyber world.

5

Attack

Jacob, Wayne, Wade and I were pretty content after we got to Logan's Fort. We hadn't had a chance to start finding and staking out our claims but we knew our time would come. Meanwhile, we were able to rest easier inside the fort walls, eat food cooked by a woman and Jacob was able to help me with reading.

I could read a little and might have been able to read more if I'd had more material to read. It turned out that Jacob had a bunch of letters he had received from men all over the American colonies, I mean states. These letters told Jacob what the feeling of the people in the area was and why they felt that way. I didn't always agree with what the writer wrote and questioned some of the letters. Jacob's response was that sometimes understanding the why of an opinion was more important than whether the man's opinion was right or wrong. I wasn't convinced but I reckoned that Jacob knew what he was talking about.

"Hugh," Jacob told me, "sometimes you need to let a man have his say and then work on coming up with something you can both live with."

I didn't really understand it then. I understand it better now and I reckon that if I understood it as good as Jacob, that I'd have got as rich as he did.

We felt pretty safe inside the fort walls. When anyone had to go outside the gates, guards went with them. If a man was working outside the fort, another man was standing guard. Sometimes they would swap off the working and the guarding.

Now it goes without saying that if the women had to leave the fort, guards went with them. For Indians to capture women-folk would be a big success. They could threaten them with torture, rape, or death if the fort wasn't surrendered. You can believe the women were guarded real good.

We were careful. We were alert. We were on guard. We were still surprised when the calm of a beautiful May morning was interrupted by the sighting of Shawnee.

First we began seeing Shawnee at a distance. We didn't see many and didn't see more than a few together at a time. Jacob suggested we slip out of the fort in the darkness and try to ambush them.

One night when the moon was clouded over, we made our way from the fort to the Flat Licks and set up an ambush. It had seemed like a good plan and a good place to set up an ambush but no one had told the Shawnee because they didn't come close to the ambush site.

It was shortly afterwards that we received a rider with news about Fort Boonesborough. He related that the fort there was under siege and had suffered a few casualties. One of the casualties was Daniel Boone who had been wounded in the ankle, or had hurt his ankle, I never did get it straight. The messenger said that if a man named Simon Butler[8] hadn't picked up Boone and carried him into the fort, that Boone would have been killed or captured.

The messenger also told us that a letter had been found tied to the scalped and mutilated body of a settler. The letter stated that any settler who swore allegiance to the king would not be attacked and would receive two hundred acres of free land. The fort was harassed beginning in March. In mid-April, there was a savage attack on Boonesborough that lasted two days. Two days of unrelenting attempts to gain an advantage over the fort's defenders were made before the Shawnee fell back. They did hot leave but stayed near the fort. Keeping enough warriors in the vicinity to harass any settlers who tried to leave the fort long enough to work their fields or even to hunt. Then those inside the fort thought they had been left alone. In late April, several men left the fort to work their fields. Fortunately, they were alert for trouble. The Shawnee attacked. After receiving only a nominal defense from the settlers, the Shawnee faked a retreat hoping to draw their pursuers into a trap. It almost worked. Seven settlers were wounded in the ensuing fight. The Shawnee maintained a close siege on Fort Boonesborough for three days and held the fort under their control for almost a month. Just before they arrived at Logan's Fort, the Shawnee killed all the settlers' livestock they could find and attempted to fire the fort. The final fighting left another three fort defenders killed.

The messenger told us that while there were still Shawnee around Boonesborough, most of them had gone. It was no mystery to us where the Shawnee had gone. They were surrounding us.

---

[8] Simon Butler was the alias used by Simon Kenton when he thought he was running from the charge of murder.

The Shawnees are fierce warriors. They are among the most feared and respected of the Ohio Indians in the Ohio Valley. We knew that we were in for a hard fight if they attacked us.

The Shawnee had been living in the Ohio Valley as far back as the late 1600s. The Iroquois Nation claimed this land and did not want to share with the Shawnee. The Ohio Valley was rich hunting grounds so the Iroquois drove the Shawnees out. The Shawnee spread from Illinois to Pennsylvania, Maryland, Georgia, and even had a village in Kentucky north and east of where Boonesborough was founded. No Shawnee had been living in Kentucky since before the French and Indian War. As the ambition and warrior power of the Six Nations of the Iroquois grew weaker, the Shawnee returned. The set up towns and crops in the lower Scioto River valley.

The Shawnees spoke a languages of the Algonquian and were kin to the Delaware, Miami, and Ottawa. The Shawnee referred to the Wyandot as their "uncles."

As enemy of the Iroquois, the Shawnee were allies of the French. This changed when British traders moved in among with better goods and prices than the French could offer. When the French ran the British out of the Ohio Valley at the beginning of the French and Indian War, the Shawnee sided with the French. Of course, this changed when the British whipped the French. The French posts were turned into British forts. During the Pontiac Rebellion of 1763, the Shawnee and other tribes fought the British and the colonists. The Shawnee leader. Cornstalk led the Shawnee against British colonists during Lord Dunmore's War in 1774. When the War for American Independence started, the British enlisted the Shawnee and other tribes to attack the Americans. The Shawnees believed the British would win and were promised that there would be no Americans allowed west of the mountains.

For ten days, we knew that there were Indians around us but they appeared to be waiting us out. We figured that if we didn't offer targets, they wouldn't have anything to shoot at. We hoped they would get bored and leave for easier pickings, which they were known to do sometimes.

That was the situation for ten days. Then suddenly, one morning, there was not a sound outside the fort and not a sign or sound on a Shawnee. No one left the fort to conduct a scout because our numbers were too small. No one was sure but people seemed to breathe easier.

After the forting up of the past twelve days, the women were beginning to feel the effects of cabin fever. They could hear the hurt bellowing of cows that needed to be milked. Feeling that it was safe, the women decided to leave the fort and milk their cows.

Several of us had gone out to guard the women while they milked the cows. Some folks that don't know no better have asked why we didn't have the milk cows in the fort with us. The answer is; of course there was not enough food and room for the milk cows. Hindsight might suggest strongly that we could have had a better arrangement but we didn't.

We did keep some horses inside the fort because they would be necessary if someone needed to travel fast. Sometimes speed was more important than milk.

We were alert and we were careful but we were still surprised when a large bunch of Shawnee came running out of the cane-brake, screaming and shooting. The suddenness and the screaming caused us to freeze up for a second but then we got busy.

I moved between the women and the Shawnee and fired an aimed shot. I think it was a good hit. I think somebody was shouting orders but I can't be sure. I did notice that the rest of the men were with me between the women and the Shawnee.

Logan hollered, "The women are safe, run for the fort."

I ran maybe five or six steps when I looked back to see what was going on behind us. When I looked back, I stepped in a hole or something and went ass over teakettle to the ground. It hurt like the dickens and at first I thought I had been shot.

I had my rifle and tried to get up. I found right then and there that my ankle was bad hurt, although there was no blood. I thought I was in one hell of a predicament, chased by shooting Shawnee and with a half loaded rifle. I had staggered maybe two steps when Wayne and Wade grabbed me and drug me through the fort gates.

They sat me down in the shade and two of the women were right there doctoring me. There wasn't much that they could do. They raised my leg up and put it on a chopping stump. It was beginning to hurt so bad that I was tempted to tell them to go ahead and chop it off.

Trying to get my mind off the pain, I asked, "Did everybody make it back inside the fort?"

"At least one, maybe two dead. One wounded and you hurt."

I started to say that given a choice, I'd rather be wounded. Good sense told me that I should keep my mouth shut. There could be a lot in worse shape than me before it got over with. Instead, I suggested, "If you could leave me with a gourd of water, I should be okay."

"I'll get you some water but you aint going to be in good shape for a while."

She emphasized her remark by squeezing my ankle just a little. It was all that I could do to keep from yelling out. She brought me water and everyone else left me alone while they took up positions at the firing holes in the fence and in the high blockhouses.

There were fifteen men defending the fort, not counting me and the other wounded. There was a total of fifteen women and children. Jane Menifee and Esther Whitley had rifles and were at adjoining firing holes. Their husbands said later that the two of them could have talked half the Shawnees outside the fort to death. Both, however, were good shots.

By early afternoon, I had been moved to a firing hole near the gate. Looking through it, I thought I saw some movement. Focusing on the movement, I saw it came from one of our fallen. At first I thought a Shawnee was trying to pull the body back so that he could scalp it. I trained my rifle just under the body and waited. Then the body moved again, but it seemed to be trying to crawl toward the fort. I started to call Jacob but remembered that Jacob had been sent to one of the corner blockhouses.

"Ben Logan!"

Something in my voice must have alerted him because it wasn't half a minute before Ben Logan was bending down beside me.

"What is it Hugh?"

"I think one of our dead aint dead."

"What?"

Logan pulled my rifle out of the firing hole and stared through one side of it. While he watched, a bullet struck within two feet of the hole.

Logan didn't flinch. "They can't shoot at all," he said softly.

Logan stood up and called some of the men over. He pointed out that Harrison (for that was the man's name) was only wounded and had not been killed.

Logan then made a plea for a rescue party. "Men, if the

Shawnee see him move, the Shawnee will try to scalp him. All it will take is two, maybe three of us, to go get him."

At first there was silence. Then the silence was interrupted by Harrison's wife, "What is wrong with you men? Can't you see he needs help out there? Why don't you go get him?"

The men with Logan shifted about. You could tell that they were uncomfortable. You could also tell that none of them really wanted to risk their own life to save Harrison. I could understand how they felt and couldn't blame them. Truth be told, I was suddenly grateful for my sprained ankle because no one could expect me to try to run out and carry Harrison back.

Don't mistake our fear as our being unable or unwilling to fight. We had all proven that we could and would fight but rescuing Harrison seemed like a suicide mission. The trouble was, Harrison's wife wouldn't let up.

"What is wrong with all you men? Can't you see that he needs help out there? Why don't you go get him?"

There was no answer to her plea except the crying of her children. I tried to step forward but the pain reminded me quick that I was, for the time being, a cripple.

Ben Logan leaned his rifle against the wall and placed his powderhorn and pouch beside it. He removed anything that would be extra weight and asked, "Who'll go with me."

A man named John Martin stepped up and answered, "I'll go with you."

Martin started placing his rifle and gear against the wall when another woman started raising a ruckus. Martin's wife ran up and threw herself on him, hugging him tight and crying. Between sobs she begged, "Don't go, don't go, don't go, don't go, don't go, don't go."

Outside the fort, Harrison tried to raise himself up. Ben Logan didn't wait. He grabbed a bale of wool and rushed to Harrison. Reaching the wounded man, Logan tried to keep them both low and help the man crawl to the gate. Harrison, due either to pain, weakness, or both could not move to the fort. He fainted or passed out. Logan pulled the wounded man up and putting his arms around the man's chest, began to pull him toward the fort gates.

Photo by Jim Cummings graphicenterprises.net

The Shawnee, seeing the rescue began firing from the cover of the canebrakes. We could hear the shots and hear the lead balls hitting the fort but we could not see a single Shawnee. I tried to find a target but the closest I could come to finding one was the black powder smoke curling out of the canebrake. Several of our men fired back but they didn't have a visible target to aim at. I figured that some were shooting out of frustration and the idea that they should be doing something, even if it was just make noise. Just the same, they kept up a heavy fire until Logan and Harrison got through the gate and inside the fort.

Logan staggered through the gate with Harrison. Even I, from where I stood at a firing hole, could tell Harrison was hit real bad. As far as Mrs. Harrison was concerned, her husband was inside the fort and he was safe. I wasn't going to be the one to tell her different if I could help it.

Right then, there was no time to tell anyone anything. The Shawnees were right put off at having an easy scalp stolen from right beneath their knives and tomahawks. Before Logan and Harrison were fully through the gates, waves of Shawnee were charging the fort. They started shooting before they even got close. We could hear the lead balls beating on the fort walls. The area around the gates was pummeled by lead. The attack didn't let up. The handful of us in the fort were kept busy defending against a violent and furious assault. It seemed to me that the attacking Shawnee were eaten up with an uncontrollable rage. Our numbers had been reduces to fourteen and a half men (with my bad ankle I couldn't count myself as being more than half a man) against over two hundred Shawnee. Two hundred Shawnee that were rabies mad. That bunch was determined to take the fort and kill or capture everyone inside. We were just as determined that they wouldn't. The Shawnee attacked, lost men, regrouped and attacked again. They swarmed at the fort like hornets leaving a kicked nest and we fired at them as fast as we could.

The women were a big help. They were reloading trade guns, muskets and rifles just as fast as they could. Every time a bunch of Shawnee got close, I'd cut loose with a trade gun loaded with .30 caliber balls. Other men were doing the same. If the men weren't shooting fast enough, one of the women would step up and unload a load of buckshot at the Shawnee.

We, the men and women in the fort, fought the over two hundred Shawnee attacking us. The Shawnee were drunk with blood lust and blind with rage. I began to wonder if they were whiskey drunk too. That would have explained the continuous attacks. The Shawnee swarmed up the hill, and again and again only to have to retreat in confusion before the continuous deadly firing from the fort. I don't know how long the attacks lasted. At least two hours, possibly three or four hours. However long it was, they failed to capture the fort. When they finally drug their dead off the field of battle and disappeared into the cane brake, I was damn glad to see them go. I couldn't remember ever having been so thirsty.

Everyone else seemed to feel the same and several were already guzzling gourds of water. I soon joined them.

We cleaned the guns and reloaded them. We made paper cartridges for the trade guns and fowlers. The women were molding bullets and two men were knapping flints into sharpness.

We waited and watched but no further attacks came that day or night.

We waited and watched but no further attacks came that day or night

6

THE SIEGE

Nobody inside the fort slept soundly that night.

Some of us barely slept at all. We should have got more sleep but after the battle we had been through, we didn't get much sleep. We did try to get some sleep. Ben Logan divided us into two watches so half the men would be asleep and the other half awake and on watch at any given time. I did doze for a couple of hours early in the evening and another hour closer to morning but that was all. I don't think anyone else got much more sleep than I did.

Just before daybreak, the women started cooking a meal. There was no milk this morning and, as far as we knew, no milk cows left alive. We figured we wouldn't have any livestock left when the Shawnee were finished.

Worse yet, Bill Hudson had been killed and scalped and two men John Kennedy and Burr Harrison) were too bad wounded to help defend the fort.   Like Jacob said, we'd have to do the best we could with what we had. Right then, it didn't seem like we had an awful lot.

I wasn't feeling real good about myself either. I hadn't been wounded but my ankle and foot were swollen so bad that I couldn't put on a moccasin or pull on a pair of breeches or leggings over them. Part of me thought I might be in better shape if I had been wounded instead of spraining my ankle, but I knew that was foolishness.

I had already learned, and relearned since, is that there is always somebody somewhere that is worse off than you are. That may not make a lot of sense to some folks but it sure has been proved to be true for me more than once. I reckon it don't do a body a bit of good to feel sorry for themselves.

Right then, I didn't know who to feel the sorrier for. It was a tossup between Bill Hudson's widow who was suffering the death of her husband and Burr Harrison's wife who was (in all likelihood) watching her husband die. I reckoned that self-pity over a bad ankle sprain was way down on my list.

Ben Logan passed among us while we watched from the wall, guarding against a surprise dawn attack. The women were carrying food and water to us. He paired us up so that one person could rest while the other watched. I say person because Esther Whitley was staying beside her husband, Billy and Jane Menifee was staying real close to her husband. It was a known fact that both those women were dead on shots.

Wayne and Wade were together and I was paired with Jacob. I took first watch and Jacob settled down with his pipe. Jacob enjoyed his pipe but he never smoked it while we were on the trail. He said the tobacco scent carried pretty far and that Indians could trail it back to the pipe. He may have been right.

There was a lot about Jacob that I didn't know. I decided to find out a little more before I got much older.

"Jacob," I asked, "where did you get the idea of wrapping buckshot and powder in paper to make loading quicker?"

"Up north, during the French and Indian War."

Now that sure surprised me. I had no idea that Jacob had ever been up north, let alone been in on the fighting up there.

"Who told you?"

"I'm not sure I remember, exactly. We were all doing it. Everyone in the bunch I was with."

"Which bunch was that?"

"We called ourselves Roger's Rangers."

"How long were you with them?"

"Only two years. Just long enough to learn a few things." He puffed on his pipe and continued, "Roberts had us prepare paper cartridges the he called 'buck and ball' cartridges. A .75 round ball and half a dozen .30 or .32 caliber round shot. Another trick we used was to cut six inches off the muzzle of our Brown Bess Muskets. This made them easier to reload."

Jacob paid attention to his pipe again, then added, "Stark used buck and ball loads at Bunker Hill."

My surprises just kept on coming. "How did you know that?"

Jacob responded to my question by removing a buckskin pouch that had been made water tight by melted wax. Unfolding the cover, he searched through pieces of paper until he found what he was searching for. He unfolded a letter and handed it to me.

A little ashamed, I suggested, "Maybe you should read it to me."

Jacob obliged. The letter was from John Stark giving an account of the Battle of Bunker Hill. Stark said that if he had another hundred men and if there had been enough powder. That the British would have been thoroughly defeated. He also suggested that Jacob come join him. Later, is an added paragraph, Stark said he had a falling out with some of the brass and was returning to Bennington, New Hampshire.

"How'd you come to be up north?"

"I was going to school."

"I didn't know that."

"Yes, my father was educated and he wanted me to be educated?"

"I don't know much about your father. I've heard that he wrote a lot of letters and got a lot of letters."

"My father was an educated man. A man of ideas who believed it was better to have his money work for him than for him to work for money."

Jacob reloaded and lit his pipe before continuing, "He said he loved my mother from the first time he saw her. She was from Delaware and was indentured to a family in Cambridge Massachusetts.

"I remember your mama. She had yellow hair and folks said she was from someplace else."

"Her family came from Sweden. The Swedes were the first settlers over here to build houses out of logs. Delaware got its name from Delaware Bay, which received its name from Lord De la War who died onboard a ship in the bay. The first settlement in Delaware was of Swedes and Finns. They came from Sweden in 1638. My mother's people came from the Swedes who first came over. As she told it, her family was large with a lot of daughters. Her father indentured his older daughters out to make money to educate the sons, raise the younger daughters and invest for their dowries."

The idea of indenturing or bounding someone was not new to me. Most of the Scots-Irish[9] who came to the colonies came as indentured servants. It was also not unusual to 'bound' a child to someone so they could learn a trade or to pay off a debt owed by the father. I had never given it a lot of thought. It was just the way that things were done. As Jacob continued talking, I gave it more thought.

"My father went to the man who held her papers. He offered to buy her indenture. The man wanted to make a profit. My father offered to work in the man's business to pay the extra the man wanted. The man insisted that my father indenture himself to the man. My father was cautious. He talked to a friend whose father practiced Law and the friend's father looked at the papers. He then rewrote them in a way that protected my father. Both my father and the business man signed the papers."

"What did that change?"

"The man first decided to deny permission for my mother to wed. When it was pointed out to him that the language of the contract nullified the contract if this happened. He then tried to sell first, my mother's indenture and then my father's indenture. Each

---

[9] Sometimes referred to as Scotch-Irish.

time he was shown that these actions violated the contract. Then my father's actions at his business saved him from a huge loss. Afterwards, he quit trying to manipulate the situation and released my mother from her indenture. He also began paying my father a salary and teaching him the business. The end result was that everyone profited."

"Aside from getting his wife, how did your father profit?"

"He learned to invest money and make a profit. He taught me a lot and saw to it that I received an education."

I started to ask Jacob why he spent so much time hunting but didn't. I remembered that he was supposed to have been married once and that his wife had died in childbirth.

"Hugh, there are three things a man must learn to do. First, he needs to learn how to make money. Second, he needs to learn how to save money. Third, he needs to learn how to make his money work for him."

Jacob puffed on his pipe for a moment and added, "Making money is usually the easiest of the three."

There at the fort wall, sitting on makeshift benches, we talked. Mostly Jacob talked and I listened. Some of what he told me I already knew, but it made more sense the way he said it. Some of it, I had never thought about but the way Jacob explained it made it seem worth thinking about.

That was the way we passed the time. Him talking and teaching and me listening and learning. We knew the Indians were still there because they taunted us from just out of rifle range. There were no more all out, full scale attacks which was a blessing. Fighting off the first attacks had left us bad short on gunpowder.

Ben Logan paired us up so that one person could rest while the other watched.

7

RELIEF

Except for conversation, our stay in the fort was largely being tired, half fed and bored. Ben briefed us on the food situation. There was food in the fort but not enough to withstand a long siege. To add to the problem, if we let the Shawnee know we were having to ration food, it would encourage them to continue the siege until they starved us out. In an attempt to fool them, we added more wood to the cook fire and acted like we were celebrating.

It was a tense time. We had reinforced the gate with extra poles and placed chopping axes next to the gate. We knew that if the walls were ever breached or any Shawnee managed to get over the walls that we were in trouble. The Shawnee did their best to catch us unaware so they could take advantage of our carelessness.

While we were pretending to have feasts and celebrate, the Shawnee feasted on the livestock they had killed and celebrated loudly. They were usually careful to stay out of rifle range but sometimes we got lucky.

Overall, the days of the siege were tiresome and boring. It got to the point where I would have welcomed an attack just for a change. Given that our powder was pretty low, it's a good thing the

Shawnee did not attack. We were low on just about everything, powder, food and patience.

We knew we were in trouble and had no idea of how to fix it short of sending someone to the settlements for supplies. Both Harrodsburg and Boonesborough were in a little better shape than we were but did not have any men to spare to bring any extra ammunition to us. Truth to tell, there were a sight of Shawnee between us and Fort Harrod and a sight of Shawnee between us and Fort Boonesborough.

Then one morning, after about two weeks, there was no sign of the Shawnee. We watched, we waited and eventually some men went outside the gates for a cautious scout of the area. There was no sign that any Shawnee were in the area.

We all knew the Fort needed gunpowder. There was plenty of gunpowder in Kentucky. George Rogers Clark had made a trip to Virginia and had persuaded Virginia governor Patrick Henry to send gunpowder and lead to Kentucky. Meeting with Governor Patrick Henry, Clark convinced him to create Kentucky County, Virginia. Governor Henry also appointed Clark a major in the Virginia Militia. Clark returned with the gunpowder and lead in the dead of winter. The problem was at any given time, two of Kentucky's three forts would be tied down by the Shawnee. It was hard enough for a single messenger to sneak through. It would be almost impossible for a man carrying gunpowder and lead to pass un-noticed.

Ben Logan did not waste any time. He selected Jacob and one other to go with him and they started for the gap and points east. Like I mentioned before; keeping some horses inside the fort was a necessary action and a good idea. No one believed the Shawnee had completely departed. A few days later, after making sure those of us who stayed would be as safe as possible, the trio rode out during a storm attempting to reach the Holston and resupply.

Leaving, the three men passed unseen by Shawnee who were more interested in staying out of the severe thunderstorm than searching for scalps. They made their way through Cumberland Gap, to Martin's Station and there they separated. Ben Logan went for supplies and Jacob, who had received personal information at Martin's Station; turned south into North Carolina. I never did hear of what happened to the third man.

When Ben reached his destination, he loaded himself down with supplies, powder and lead. He attempted to recruit reinforcements but was not successful. He was able to send a messenger to the Virginia government with a detailed report of the alarming Indian problems in Kentucky. With this accomplished, he headed back to Kentucky.

Logan's trip back was perilous and dangerous to the extreme. The storms continued and the combination of heavy rains and swollen rivers and creeks made it difficult to protect the gunpowder. He almost drowned crossing the Rockcastle River. The last fifty miles, he was dodging and evading the Shawnee.

Logan left the Trace and made his way south of Logan's Fort, and approached the fort from the west. Approaching the fort at night during a storm, he was able to reach the gate before the Shawnee could stop him.

Entering the fort, he handed off the pack horses to others and gathered his family in his embrace. Seeing him alone I became over whelmed with worry about Jacob. I waited for Ben to get comfortable before I approached him.

Nodding at me, Ben said, "Hugh, Jacob got some news at Martin's Station and had to go down to North Carolina to take care of some things. He said for you to rest your leg and to help defend the fort until he gets back."

"Did he say what was wrong?"

"No. I guess he didn't want to add to my worries. He said to expect him by August."

"August? What is the date now?"

"June, I think."

"June 25th 1777," interrupted his wife Ann.

The rest of June and weeks into July, most of our time was spent inside the walls of the fort. Sometimes we saw the Shawnee. I don't know which was worse, when we saw the Shawnee or when we didn't see the Shawnee. I guess it didn't matter because we knew that they were outside the fort, hiding in canebrakes or forest.

The inside of the fort had changed. Burr Harrison had died on June 13 and was buried inside the fort. That left the fort with two widows and several orphans. Given the scarcity of women in the country, the women probably wouldn't be widows long. There were at least ten white men in Kentucky for every white woman and most of the eligible women were married. Esther Whitley had even mentioned to me that Harrison's widow would be a good catch. I don't know what it is about women but they seem to be bound and determined to get every woman without a man married off just as soon as they can.

Shortly after Ben returned, we heard that both Fort Harrod and Fort Boonesborough had been continually harassed by Indians. The Indians hadn't killed many settlers but they had killed all the livestock that they could find. The Shawnee were able, apparently, to focus on a fort while leaving enough warriors at the other two forts to keep everyone on their toes.

I noticed, when scouting around the fort, that the number of Shawnee besieging the fort seemed to change on almost a daily basis. I talked to Ben Logan about my thoughts and he too speculated that the Shawnee were keeping all three forts in

Kentucky under their control by shifting large bodies of Shawnee among the forts while always leaving a large enough force to prevent an easy breakout by the occupants of the fort.[10]

Forting up was never a pleasure but it was sometimes a necessity. After a while, people began to feel like they were more captive than protected. Still, it was probably better to be alive and feel like a prisoner than to be killed or captured, scalped and mutilated, or possibly tortured.

The women were the quickest to lose their tempers with each other. The men knew that if they pushed someone too far that there would have to be a fight and then either they might have to kill the other person or be killed. Women, because they had been largely protected, were quicker to lose their tempers and force an issue. They also were quicker to use gossip and slander as a weapon.

Fortunately, the women at Logan's fort kept that down to a loud purr instead of letting it grow to a full roar. The women were strong and equally as important, sensible. Forting up was hard on everyone's nerves.

It was still risking a man's life to venture far from a fort. Sometimes it wasn't safe to try to get to a fort. At Logan's Fort, we received word that a settler named Daniel Lyon had headed to join us and no one had heard anything about him since. Some men out scouting found a piece of a leather hunting shirt that was thought to belong to him. These same men reported lots of Indian sign.

There was a lot of Indian sign. I don't think any of the three forts was ever completely abandoned by the Shawnee. All three forts were kept under surveillance, but by different numbers of

---

[10] After the Siege of Fort Harrod was lifted, a camp that had sheltered over 500 Shawnee was located less one quarter of a mile from Fort Harrod but was completely out of sight of the fort.

Shawnee. Our thought was that if a fort ever looked too relaxed, that fort would get attacked.

We got news from a messenger in mid-July that Colonel Bowman was on his way with a hundred men. We later learned that six men sent ahead by Bowman to tell Logan that help was on the way were attacked. Andrew Gressom was killed and scalped, and Jones Mannifee and Samuel Ingram were badly wounded.

Finally, around the end of July, Bowman and his men arrived at Logan's Fort. Several of us gathered outside the gate to welcome the relief force. With the arrival of reinforcements, Logan's Fort and possibly the whole of Kentucky was saved from the Shawnee.

Several of us gathered outside the gate to welcome the relief force.

8

CHANGES

We stood outside the gates and waited for Bowman and his men to reach us. Now we were all damn glad to see them but we were tired and didn't go crazy with greetings until Ben came out and got us all stirred up.

"Alright, men, three huzzahs for Colonel Bowman and his men!"

Well, if Ben wanted us to huzzah, we'd huzzah. We shouted out our huzzahs but the last one kind of failed on me when I saw that Jacob was with them. Jacob was with them and he was with a woman!

"Jacob!"

I walked, well kind of limped, out to meet him and grab him by the hand. I'd missed him and wasn't sure I would ever see him again. I didn't know what to think about him bringing out a woman. I figured that Jacob had found a wife. I also didn't know how a wife would affect discussing his letters and politics. Women could

73

sometimes mess with things like that.

I glanced at her and saw that the woman was a tiny little thing with a large shawl hiding her hair, face and shoulders. I decided right off that she was too puny for the Kentucky frontier. Still and all, I wasn't going to get anywhere criticizing Jacob's new wife.

Figuring I would take the bull by the horns, I asked, "Jacob where did you find your new wife?"

Hearing my words, the wife moved from a slouch to sitting straight up. The shawl fell back showing that she was just a girl with blue eyes, smooth skin and soft looking yellow hair. It was her eyes that caught me. They looked clear and deep, deep enough to swim in. The blue of her eyes seemed to darken as a blush reddened her whole face.

"Wife?"

I was glad that Jacob decided to take over. "Hugh, this is my daughter Sarah. Sarah, this is my good friend Hugh Mason.

I removed my hat and nodded by head at Sarah. I had heard that Jacob had a daughter but I didn't know of anyone who had ever seen her. I wondered what Jacob was doing bringing a twelve year old daughter into the Kentucky Wilderness. As Sarah started to dismount her horse, at least a dozen of Bowman's men rushed over to help. I started to step away but when Jacob moved to her side, I moved with him.

Facing the Militiamen, Jacob said, "I told you men already to keep your distance and stop pestering her."

The militiamen stepped back and Jacob helped her off the horse. She had apparently been riding for a while because she was a little unsteady and touched my arm to steady herself. I instinctively held her shoulder and hand to help her steady herself.

That was all it took. Her touch and my hands on her hit me like a bolt of lightning. I was suddenly aware that I was gunpowder stained and hadn't changed my buckskins since arriving at Logan's Fort. In fact, except for having to slit my leggings when I sprained my ankle, I hadn't changed clothes since the Indians started besieging the fort. I also realized that she was not a twelve year old girl.

As the other single men from the fort started gathering, Jacob told us, "Let's go" and led us to Ann Logan.

"Ann, this is my daughter Sarah, can she stay in your cabin?"

"Oh my goodness, Jacob, I didn't know you had a daughter. Why of course, she can stay."

"Ann, if any of these bachelors come calling, let them know she is done spoke for."

Ann Logan's eyes widened and she smiled. "Of course Jacob, who is the lucky young man?"

Jacob shifted about a little before answering, "I aint talked to her about it yet."

"Do you mean she hasn't told you?"

"No, I mean I've not told her yet"

With that, Jacob turned and began to walk swiftly away. I followed. He didn't stop until he got to their horses and began to unsaddle and unpack them. I decided to wait for him to speak.

We finished unsaddling and unpacking the horses. Jacob picked up a brush and began brushing a horse down. I found a brush and went to work on the pack horse. I continued to wait for Jacob to speak. After Jacob was finished with the first horse and had started on the second, he finally spoke;

"I reckon you got some questions on how Sarah got to be out here with us?"

"No."

"I reckon you wonder how we are going to manage with a woman out here with us."

"No."

"I reckon you're some put out at the extra trouble we are going to have?"

"No."

"I reckon you want to know how she come to be out here with us."

"Yes."

Jacob continued brushing the second horse as he spoke. "Sarah was staying with my sister. She's been with my sister since, well all of her life."

I noticed that Jacob didn't say since his wife died. The story I had heard was that his wife had died during childbirth. This in itself was not unusual. A great many women died during childbirth. Times were rough and less than half of all babies survived their first year. I still didn't figure it was time for me to talk yet.

"When we got to Martin's Station, I saw a man who knows both me and my sister. He told me that a man from a Tory family was giving unwelcome attention to Sarah. I went to take care of it but he was warned and went into hiding, the cowardly son of a bitch. I figured it was either I stayed there or I brought her with me."

"So you brought her to Kentucky."

"Yes. Maybe it was a bad idea?"

"No. It was a good idea."

"I was afraid you wouldn't like the idea of us making our place with the responsibility of a half grown girl to watch out after."

"Jacob, she's almost a woman and as soon as she's grown and as soon as I have a working place of my own, I aim to marry her."

"Ooooh damn, not you too. At least half of Bowman's men want to ask her. I told Bowman I would kill any man who pestered her."

It goes without saying that Jacob had a problem. Unmarried women were scarce on the Kentucky frontier. I expected both widows in the fort to be married within a month or two. There wasn't much of a place for an unmarried woman or a widow with no children big enough to take care of her. Their choices were either to indenture themselves to a family, return to east of the mountains or get a husband. Usually, it was easier to get a husband. Even before Colonel Bowman and nigh on to a hundred militiamen came to Kentucky, single men outnumbered single women by at least ten to one. Come to think of it, it might have been closer to fifteen to one or better.

I figured it was time for me to speak. "Jacob, I'll not pester her and I don't aim to say anything to her before I have a place all set up. Like as not, I am a damn fool but I feel about her like I never felt about anybody else. If I'd a felt this way before, I'd have done been hitched."

"Hugh, you make sure that you feel that way and have your own place set up. After that, you need to convince her. My sister says that she is strong minded."

"I'll work on that."

We started to go wash up and make ourselves more presentable. We weren't the only ones with that idea. Every man who wasn't on picket duty was trying to wash and shave. Jacob led me to a creek he knew about and while I stood guard for Shawnee, he washed and put on linen breeches and a linen shirt. Then he stood guard while I washed. I've got to admit that I felt better. When I got out of the creek, Jacob had linen breeches and a linen shirt for me to wear. I tied my long hair back with a buckskin thong, slipped on moccasins and we were ready to go.

We went straight to Logan's cabin and Jacob knocked on the door. To get to the door, we had to go past seventeen men who were waiting for someone to open the door and ask them to come in. Ben, himself, opened the door.

"Jacob, Jacob, come on in. You come in too Hugh. Jacob, I have been wanting to ask you how feelings are in North Carolina."

"Ben, everybody is waiting for the next man to jump. The patriots are on top right now but not by much. The Tories figure that if they wait it out the King's army will win and they can take whatever they want from everyone else."

Ann Logan brought us mugs of rum and water. "That is pretty much what Sarah told me. You have a sharp daughter there Jacob. How long do you think you can keep a man from running off with her?"

"A while, anyway."

"Jacob, as long as she is not married, men are going to be fighting over her and not paying attention to their duty. Furthermore, the married women won't want an unmarried woman tempting their men."

Jacob's face got red with anger. "Sarah wouldn't -------"

"Jacob, I know that but some wives aint got a lick of sense and you know as well as I do that some men would be tempted by a woman's footprint in dirt."

The red in Jacob's face turned from anger to embarrassment. He didn't speak.

"Jacob, all those unmarried militiamen are in a big hurry to start courting. What are we going to do?"

Before Jacob could form an answer, Sarah walked over and placed her hands on Jacob's shoulders. I had the idea that she was upset and was going to let us all know about it, but she surprised me. She spoke to us as sweet and nice as honey or cane sugar.

"The answer," she said, "is simple. We will just tell everyone that I am spoken for and they will leave me alone."

Ann Logan was the first to respond. "That just might work. But, just who can we say she is betrothed with? Who would go along with that story?"

"Well," Jacob said in his most reflective tone, "I reckon Hugh will do it to help us out. He owes me a few favors."

It was my turn to turn red and speechless. Everyone was suddenly looking at me and I felt that I should say something. Instead of speaking, I took a swallow of my rum and water and like to strangled on it.

"Hugh," Sarah was saying my name in that sweeter than honey or sugar voice, "would you do me that little favor?"

I wondered if she was teasing me or maybe just having a little fun with me. I started to give just the sort of answer that such teasing would deserve but I caught myself. I figured 'damn the consequences,' I'd answer truthful and honest.

"Ma'am, if you asked me too, I'd chop every tree in Kentucky."

"But I know it will be such a hardship."

"No, it won't. Because I aim to take that time to make sure you know that I am the very man you need to make a life with. You are going to see that I am a hard worker and am a man you can depend on to do what is right."

"Are you sure?"

"Yes ma'am, I'm sure. From the first time you touched my arm to steady yourself, from the first time I looked into your eyes, I have never felt that way before about anyone. I think we are meant to be together and I want to make sure I am good enough for you."

She stepped closer to me. She leaned over and squeezed my hand, then walked over to the table and busied herself with the food.

9

SETTLING IN

Not right away, but within a few days, Jacob and I were out scouting for a likely place to settle. We had helped scout the area and still found fresh sign that the Shawnee were still in the area. I hated to leave Sarah, but I had told her that I was going to prove myself worthy of her and I decided that mooning around like a lost calf wasn't going to prove anything. So Jacob and I scouted for a place to settle in and make a home on.

We wanted to be close to the fort but not so close that we would be on a game trail that Indians would be likely to travel on frequently. Far away enough that it wouldn't be land already claimed. Lastly, it had to be land that we could make a go of it on.

The last part was the easiest. Kentucky was full of rich soil on rolling acres of canebrakes and forest. Streams and even springs were plentiful.

Like a preacher is supposed to have said, "Let me tell you my honey's, Heaven is a Kentucky kind of place."

Where we were, the land was green and rolling. The steep

mountains were east of us. We could walk for hours without tiring. This was a big difference from the effort that climbing high hills and mountains required. Everything was beautiful. It almost seemed a shame to ruin it by settling on it and turning the paradise we explored into farmland. I said as much to Jacob.

Jacob gazed at the forest around us before he answered.

"Hugh, I understand what you are saying and what you feel. I feel about the same way. It may be hard to believe, but there may come a day when people will look back and say they wished the farms were still here instead of what things will be like someday."

"What do you mean?"

"Benjamin Franklyn wrote first to my father and then to me about towns in England. The prettier the region, the more people try to make them prosperous. The more prosperous they get, the bigger they get. The bigger they get, the dirtier they get. The dirtier they get, the less beautiful they are."

I had never studied about that predicament at all. I stayed quiet as I thought about what Jacob had said. For a minute, I was ready to tell Jacob that we should go back east of the mountain and leave the paradise that was Kentucky alone. I was tempted but I couldn't do it. I wanted to wake up and step outside to work on Kentucky land. I wanted my sons to learn to love and appreciate Kentucky like I did. I wanted to build a life for myself and my family in this Kentucky paradise.

The truth was, where we settled would be an island in the Kentucky wilderness. The advance of the settlement of the Kentucky frontier was not a smooth, steady movement from east to west. There were areas still in Virginia that were unsettled but were owned. A landless settler didn't want to start making a home at the edge of a settlement. He wanted to travel to find a place where the land was better to make his home. He wanted a place that no one else had any claim on. He wanted a place of his own to pass on to his sons. The settler wanted land like this section of Kentucky, not a farm on the side of a mountain that would work him into an early grave and never be profitable. Certain places, like the cane fields the middle of Kentucky were desired above the more rugged areas.

Bypassing the more rugged land was a good idea. Dr. Thomas Walker entered Kentucky and named Cumberland Gap, the Cumberland Mountains and the Cumberland River. He was not very impressed about what he discovered in his explorations. He explored a lot of rough country but if he had traveled fifteen to twenty miles further west before turning north, he would have found land that was less rugged, far richer, and much more desirable.

Settlers bypassed a lot of territory to claim land in the middle of Kentucky. James Harrod and his companions traveled sixty miles to the Ohio River and over 500 miles down the Ohio and Kentucky rivers to settle on the headwaters of the Salt River. Daniel Boone led a party of settlers over 250 miles through the Mountains to build new homes around Boonesborough? Hancock Taylor left Virginia, and traveled over 700 miles to claim land for himself at the falls of the Ohio and on Elkhorn Creek? Why did George Rogers Clark leave his land claim on the upper Ohio and moved to Leestown? Each of these men could have settled for land much closer to their homes. The available land was a lot closer but was not what these pioneers wanted.

On one hand, I wanted to find the best place to build a life for Sarah. On the other hand, I would have been happy about anyplace as long as she was with me.

We finally settled on a likely spot and began tomahawking our claim. To do this, we blazed trees around the area we wanted to claim. Jacob took notes of the land and its peculiarities on every corner of our claim.

After marking our claim, we copied all of Jacob's notes and left them with Ben Logan. There was no place except the Transylvania Land Office to register a claim and Jacob didn't believe they would last long. Jacob did not believe that Virginia would honor Richard

Henderson and the Transylvania Company claims to Kentucky.

Sarah stayed with the Logan's family while Jacob and I built a crude shelter and girdled trees. As a gesture of establishing our claim, we planted a plot of corn but we didn't expect much of a crop. The planting was symbolic. After all, it was already August.

Our first shelter was a three sided lean-to that measured twelve by twelve. It was designed so that it could be extended and attached to a cabin.

Jacob and I spent over two hours each day exploring our land and the surrounding areas. We wanted to be so familiar with our land that anything amiss would shout out a warning to us. We saw no one for the first three weeks. That changed when three white men appeared at dusk.

"Halloo the camp."

"Come on in."

While the three walked to us, Jacob moved so that a tree was covering his back and his fowler was in his hands. He leaned back against the tree. His rifle was beside him. I moved to a point where I could cover his flank and where my back was protected.

"You have no idea how glad we are to find white men. We were lost."

Jacob grinned and asked, "How did that happen?"

"We got separated from our party and tried to get ahead of them. We didn't make it."

It was easy to see and smell why they didn't make it. They were sweating whiskey and still partially drunk. It was a miracle that they hadn't ran into hostiles and been killed.

"Where were you bound?"

"Fort Harrod."

"If you look under that blanket yonder you'll find a jug of good rum. Just the thing for getting over getting lost. Fort Harrod is way to the north of here. Were you figuring on settling near there?"

"No, our friend is going after a woman. A woman who is real beautiful and who is real rich."

Jacob pretended to take a long drink of rum and passed the jug back to the visitors. They each took a long swallow.

Keeping his voice even and casual, Jacob asked, "Why would he be going to Fort Harrod to find a woman."

"Didn't you hear me say she is real beautiful and real rich? He had his sights set on her down in North Carolina but she ran off to Kentucky. Martin don't aim to let her get away though. Martin always gets what he wants and like I said, that woman is worth a whole lot of money."

"Well, that's sure the kind of woman to go after. How much money is she worth?"

I watched the three men as I listened to Jacob. He seemed calm enough but I had spent enough time with him to know that he was tense. I figured the best move to make right then was to separate the three and distract them. I tossed a pebble into an empty kettle and waited until the pinging stopped.

"If one of you men bring that kettle back full of water, I'll make us a good kettle of tea."

The man who had been doing all the talking nodded to one of the others. The man took a good swallow from the rum jug, then another. He leaned his rifle and gear against an oak and picked up the kettle. Before leaving, he took a final swallow from the jug.

"There's a spring over next to the big willow that has the best water."

The man with the kettle nodded and shifted toward the big willow and went after water.

The speaker then turned his attention to Jacob. "I'll tell you how much she is worth. She is worth a damn sight more than she knows about. Her pa is a rich man who has bought into a lot of farms and businesses. He probably don't know how much he's worth."

"Like I said, that's the kind of woman to get hitched up with. How did this Martin find out about her money?"

"Martin's pa is a banker. Martin's pa says that Jacob Hensley is one of the richest men in North Carolina."

He stared at Jacob and continued, "Maybe you know him."

"Might. There's a man named Jake up to Fort Harrod but I never thought that he was rich. He could be though. The next time I see him, I'll ask him."

"Martin figures her pa has got a big place and maybe some slaves here in Kentucky. Martin says her pa is probably the richest man in Kentucky. What's more, there is an inheritance that neither the girl nor her pa know about."

"If the girl and her pa don't know about it, how did your friend Martin find out about it?"

"Martin's pa knows a lawyer named Felton that owes his bank money. The lawyer got a letter and is holding it tight for the time being."

"Do tell."

"I tell. I tell a whole lot. There aint many as smart as Martin. He aims to be a pretty big rooster as soon as the British win." He paused long enough to make sure he was getting his share of the rum, and continued, "There aint many as smart as Martin."

I kept my face and temper still. I gathered that this was no time for an argument. Instead of flying off the handle and revealing too much, I asked, "How'd you come to get separated from this Martin?"

He was instantly on guard. He changed from talkative to cautious quicker than a bee can sting. He hesitated, glanced at his friend and the man who was almost at the spring before he answered. His answer was a question.

"How come you are drinking tea? I thought good patriots didn't drink tea."

"Just who's saying we are good patriots?"

My answer seemed to satisfy him and he grinned. "I reckon we're on the same side then. You can't be too careful. Most rebels don't wear uniforms."

I was madder than a stepped on copperhead and wanted to strike like a copperhead would. I didn't. I figured that if Jacob was staying calm that I could too. While the two were paying attention to me, Jacob straightened himself up. I could tell he was ready for anything. He still kept his back to the tree.

I spoke to keep their attention on me, "You never did say how you come to get separated from this here Martin."

The second man answered my question, "Martin needed to talk to some of his friends about a plan of his'n. They had plans to make."

The first speaker turned to the second with obvious anger, "Sometimes you talk too damn much."

"These good folks aint going to bother us none. They aint rebels and they give us some good rum."

"Damn you, shut up."

"Is something wrong?"

Jacob asked the question as innocent as a new born baby. The casual observer would not see the anger I saw beneath his friendliness and innocence.

"He just talks too much."

Both men were beginning to feel the effects of the rum. Both were beginning to show anger toward the other.

"Now look here, I won't have no fighting in this camp," commanded Jacob. "Now quit picking on him."

That is all it took. Without any further words, the two men were fighting. I moved their rifles and watched them fight. When they began to slow down, Jacob shouted, "That was not fair!"

With his shout the two men redoubled their efforts. The third man returned with the kettle of water.

"What's got into them?"

"He just attacked your friend," responded Jacob.

I passed the jug to the third man. He took a long pull and tossed back to me.

"It was awful the way he jumped your friend," Jacob told him.

The third man tried to pull the fighters apart and was dragged into the melee.

"Jacob, how strong is that rum anyway?"

"Close to a hundred percent. It was made to be mixed with equal measures of water."

"No wonder."

Within seconds, the second man was knocked out and the other two were locked in a fierce and bitter struggle. The third man was then placed in a choke hold and collapsed. The remaining man struggled upright and took the jug that was offered to him.

Jacob helped him to the shade and told him, "You just can't get good help anymore."

"'At's fer damn sure." He staggered, fell into the shade and pulled himself into a sitting position and demanded, "Water."

"First, tell me about Martin's plan."

"How'd you know about Martin's plan?"

"You were telling me when the other two jumped you. Remember?"

"Uh, Yeah, I guess."

"You were going to tell me about Martin's plan."

"Martin's plan. Yeah, it's a good plan."

"What is it?"

"Martin's got some Chickamauga to steal the girl. They steal her and Martin rescues her. Then, with her pa being dead, she goes with Martin.

"How does her pa get dead?"

"The Chickamauga kill him and if they can't, then we do."

"Sounds like a good plan."

"Damn good plan."

"How are they going to get the girl out of Fort Harrod?"

"They tell her that her pa is sick."

"Sounds like a damn good plan."

"It's a damn good plan."

"Where was Martin supposed to be planning with the Chickamauga?"

"Just west of the Crab Orchard, on a creek the Chickamauga know about."

"How long have you been separated from them?"

"Two days."

Jacob examined the second man who had been knocked out. He turned to the first man and told him, "You will be carrying your friend."

Jacob made a quick examination of the third man and turned again to the first man, "Right after you get through waking this one up."

Photo by Jim Cummings, graphicenterprises.net, Pioneer Times.

10

CHICKAMAUGA

In 1775, the Cherokee sold Kentucky to Judge Richard Henderson and the Transylvania Company. Everything went smoothly until a young chief named "Dragging Canoe" loudly objected. He stated that he would not be a party to selling the land. After he rejected the Treaty of Sycamore Shoals, Dragging Canoe declared war against all American colonists. The colonists fought back and during 1776 burned more than 50 Cherokee towns. The older Cherokee Chiefs wanted peace. Dragging Canoe, confident of help from the British, led hundreds of Cherokee to the area called Chickamauga in the Chattanooga Valley, along Chickamauga Creek. From this isolated and hard to reach area, Dragging Canoe led the Chickamauga. The bands of Chickamauga he led were comprised of Cherokees, Creeks, other Indians from other tribes, renegade whites, and escaped slaves. Supplied and armed by the British, they warred against the Carolina, Virginia, and Kentucky settlers. The Chickamauga were ever relentless in their campaign to drive settlers out of Kentucky to east of the mountains.

At the outbreak of the Revolution in 1775, the Cherokee were asked by the Mohawk, Shawnee, and Ottawa to join them in fighting the Americans. Most of the Cherokee wanted to stay neutral in the white man's war. The Chickamauga, however, were already fighting the Americans and allied with the Shawnee. Both tribes had the financial support of British Indian agents who still lived among them, usually with native wives. During 1775 the British sought help from their Indian allies by supplying them with large amounts of guns and ammunition. They also began to pay for American scalps. The Chickamauga used their gifts of guns and the incentive of payments for scalps and attacked two American forts in North Carolina. They attacked Eaton's Station and Fort Watauga. Neither attack was successful butt the raids started a series of attacks by other Cherokee and the Upper Creek on frontier settlements.

It was impossible to tell a bad Indian from a neutral Indian and the frontier militia attacked Indians where they could find them. The angry American Militia, some who had lost friends and family members, destroyed 41 Cherokee towns and killed every man, woman and child they could find. The Cherokee asked for peace and ceded most of their remaining land in the Carolinas. Because they were unable to resist the storm of outraged fury brought down on them by the actions of Dragging Canoe's Chickamauga, the Cherokee in 1777 were forced to ask for peace.

Despite the peace made between the Cherokee and the Americans, the Chickamauga continued to receive gifts from the British and continued to fight Americans.

As Jacob had noted when we were ambushed coming through the gap, Indians with new muskets were being paid by the British. The British Indian agents were making a pile of money too.

Dragging Canoe did not ask for peace. England fighting her former colonies was fine with him. He got paid to fight whites and he could sometimes manage to lay the blame on friendly

Cherokees. As long as the British viewed him as the top Chickamauga leader, he got treated real nice. He must have known that if the British lost it would just be a matter of time before the whites attacked him. Maybe he didn't know. Maybe he didn't care or maybe it didn't occur to him that the British would lose.

Jacob and I tied the three Tories on the back of a single pack horse and we all lit out for Logan's Fort. I guess that my blood was running too hot to feel any discomfort and probably Jacob was in the same state but the three Tories had a real rough ride that was made more uncomfortable by all the rum they had drunk. Neither Jacob nor me had any sympathy for them.

Jacob took us in what was almost a straight line to Logan's Fort. I noticed that he avoided well-traveled game trails and didn't slow unless he had to. When we did stop on a hill to let the horses breathe a bit, Jacob had me swing up into a giant oak and go to the top and look around. I didn't see much, just a little dust raised maybe a mile from us.

I swung down and told Jacob what I had noticed. Jacob shrugged and pointed toward the three Tories still tied on the pack horse.

"If anything happens, kill them first."

I wasn't sure that Jacob meant it but the three prisoners sure thought he meant it. One began to beg and Jacob drew his knife from its sheath.

"Any more noise and the killing starts right here."

That shut them up in a hurry. Jacob nodded to me and we put the horses into a good trot. I wanted to ride to beat Hell but I figured that Jacob was in charge and knew what he was doing. When we got to the point where I knew the fort was just over a mile away, Jacob said, "Let's go" and we went.

We rode like bats out of Hell. It wasn't fast enough. I was

kicking my poor horse and slapping it with a rope. I noticed that Jacob was treating his horse the same way.

The three Tories on the pack horse were bouncing every which a way and hollering in fright. The pack horse was trying to keep up with us but was falling behind. I was yelling myself hoarse as we got to about 250 yards from the gate. Several figures came out of the fort and aimed rifles in our direction. It was then that I heard yelling besides my own. I felt and heard the Indians behind and around us rather than saw them. Then I heard screams from the Tories who were helpless and tied to the pack horse. I glanced backwards to see their bloody bodies being pulled from the pack horse.

As we neared the gate, the group outside the gates fired a volley and pulled the gates shut behind us. Ben Logan met us as we slid off our horses.

"I hope you didn't feel obliged to bring company with you."

"We didn't."

I didn't think Jacob's answer was strong enough so I added, "Hell no we didn't."

"I was hoping we were through with the Shawnee."

"Ben," Jacob told him, "those aint Shawnee, they're Chickamauga."

"What are the Chickamauga doing up here?"

"They were hired by a man named Martin Kerry to steal Sarah."

All around us the fort was a hive of all too familiar activity. Men and guns were being stationed around the walls, buckshot filled paper cartridges were placed where they were handy and the women were preparing for another siege.

Outside the fort, the Chickamauga were brandishing the bloody scalps of the three Tories. If they hadn't been involved in a plot to steal Sarah, I might have felt sorry for them. If the Chickamauga turned the scalps in, they would be paid for them. I thought it was quite a joke that King George's Indian agents would be paying for loyalist scalps. Billy Whitley saw me grinning and came over.

"What's got you so amused?"

I told Billy the whole story. By the time I finished, he was starting to grin too.

"Well, better having them pay for loyalist scalps than ours, I guess. Maybe if we make it hard for them to get ours, they'll settle for Tory scalps."

"Maybe."

The men were upset at the hooraw the Chickamauga were making with the scalps and mutilated bodies of the Tories. As soon as we got the word around that the Indians had killed and scalped white men on their own side, the men's feelings changed.

Some men began pulling charges from their rifles and reloading them with extra care. When the charges were loaded to their satisfaction, they would point out the Indian they targeted. The target selected, the shooter would take careful aim and fire. Three shots seconds apart and three dead Chickamauga made the attackers change their strategy.

Then from the north came a volley that dropped several Chickamauga. A patrol from Colonel Bowman's militia had heard the firing and returned. The attacking Chickamauga were caught by surprise and left the field. They took the three scalps with them.

The militiamen were upset at the three scalped and mutilated bodies of the white Tories. They were kind of put out at our attitudes until we told them the whole story. They were still sickened at the barbarity the Indians had practiced on the three white men but also saw the humor of King George buying the scalps of his loyal followers.

Photo by Jim Cummings of graphicenterprises.net/pioneer times, possibly the best reenactment web site in cyberspace.

Truth to tell, there were loyalist leaning settlers in Kentucky and always had been. They didn't ever attempt to side with the British and Indians who attacked us. As long as the man was fighting against the Indians and British, we didn't care what his leaning was.

The British never came to us in Kentucky and asked which side we were on. If they had come to us and asked us to side with them and told us they would keep the Indians away from us, I don't know what the people would have decided. They didn't come to us. They didn't ask us to be part of them. They didn't offer us a choice. I guess in some ways that made it easier for us to fight them and the Indians. We didn't have any choice.

Then one of the militiamen turned to Jacob and asked, "What did you say the name of the loyalist was?"

"Martin Kerry"

"I believe that was the name of the man we ran into a couple of hours ago. He should be with Bowman now."

"Are you sure?"

"I think so. He wasn't in any mood to come to Logan's Fort. In fact he didn't know there was a Logan's Fort until Bowman told him. I think he decided to come to Logan's Fort with Bowman."

"Are you sure?"

"Yeah, pretty sure. If I'm not bad mistaken, he decided to come to Logan's Fort after he heard some of the boys talking about bringing you and your beautiful girl from North Carolina here."

"Are you saying that he knows Sarah is here?"

"I guess he does."

Jacob turned and went straight to Ben Logan.

"Ben, we got troubles here."

"Jacob, are you just now beginning to notice that?"

"Martin Kerry knows that Sarah is here."

Jacob explained to Ben what he had just learned from the militiaman. Ben's face got a sight darker as he listened but he waited until Jacob finished before he spoke.

"Jacob, what do you suggest we do?"

"If he comes in with Bowman, which I doubt, we arrest him. If he don't come in, then he's got to be hunted down."

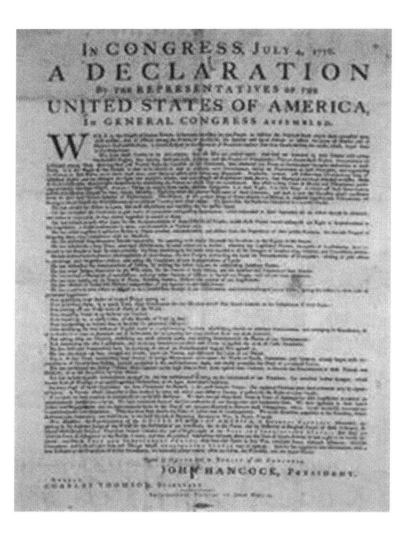

11

He has excited domestic insurrections amongst us, and has endeavoured to bring on the inhabitants of our frontiers, the merciless Indian Savages, whose known rule of warfare, is an undistinguished destruction of all ages, sexes and conditions[11]

On the Kentucky frontier, there were no 'domestic insurrections amongst us' because we were too busy dealing with 'the merciless Indian Savages, whose known rule of warfare, is an undistinguished destruction of all ages, sexes and conditions' that the British had 'endeavoured to bring on the inhabitants of our frontiers.' If the British hadn't been so all-fired in a hurry to sic their Indian dogs on us, we might have taken sides and took to fighting one another on

---

[11] Taken from the Declaration of Independence

the Kentucky frontier. We were so busy defending ourselves from the British led Indians that the politics of Patriot against Tory never really came up.

The British did accomplish one thing. They turned many Kentuckians against all Indians for a long time. A lot of us were turned against the British for a long time too.

Martin Kerry was an example of the worst kind of Tory. He was a man who used the war to enrich himself at the expense of others. I decided that no matter what happened to me, Martin Kerry was not going to get rich from Jacob and Sarah.

I slung a loaded fowler over my shoulder along with my pouch and powderhorn, picked up my rifle and went out the gate. Ever since I had heard that Jacob and Sarah had a pile of money, I was convinced that she and I did not have a future. No matter how I felt about her, I was in no position to marry her. I didn't own an acre or a plow. Be damned if I was going to have it said I didn't make it on my own and had married for money. I grabbed two militiamen and had them tell me where Bowman was likely to be and headed in that direction, alone.

Now this was not the smartest thing I had ever set out to do. It was likely that there were still Chickamauga and maybe even some Shawnee lurking about. I knew that I could be outnumbered and that my scalp was worth money to the red rascals but my anger pushed all caution aside. I stepped into the forest and moved toward where I thought I could run into Bowman and his bunch.

I would have run into them too, if they hadn't changed their direction. Bowman had decided that the force he had dispatched toward the fighting at Logan's Fort was big enough and had turned toward Fort Harrod.

I was traveling through the forest at an easy run. I could have traveled faster but I was getting myself and my anger under a little bit of control. Still, it was as much luck as anything else that I saw movement ahead of me.

I didn't slow down. I took my rifle in my left hand and drew my knife with my right. When I neared the spot where I had seen movement, I sped up and leaped at where I had seen the movement. I came down on two surprised Chickamauga warriors. Soon, blood was spurting but it was all Chickamauga blood.

One Chickamauga was cut across his neck and bled to death pretty quick but the other wasn't as lucky. I cut him in three places. The last cut was across his belly. He was still dying as I ran from the ambush spot.

I'm not real sure what got into me. Part of it was anger at the Tory who wanted to steal Sarah. I was angry that Sarah was suddenly beyond my reach because she and her father were so wealthy and part of it was the frustration of being forced to fort up so much since arriving in Kentucky.

What I was doing was foolish and reckless but sometimes foolish and reckless works. Of course, most times foolish and reckless don't work. This time foolish and reckless worked.

Covered with Chickamauga blood, I began to take stock of my situation and slowed down. Traveling in a wide circle, I carefully returned to the ambush site. The two slain Chickamauga had been joined by three live Chickamauga who were double checking the area. I think they were trying to find out how many white men had attacked the two dead Indians. It was probably beyond their understanding that one angry settler could have done such an action. Unslinging my fowler, I checked the priming and fired what I knew to be a heavy load of buck and ball at the middle Indian. The .30 caliber buckshot spread enough to nick the Indians who did not receive the main blast. Before the echo of the shot and smoke died, I shot the Indian who was furthest away with my rifle and charged the third Indian. He got one look at a blood covered demon charging out of a cloud of black powder smoke and he lit out like his ass was set afire. I yelled at him and when he looked back over his shoulder to see how close I was, he ran slap dab into a tree.

I got to the Indian as he was trying to stand up. He wasn't making a lot of progress and was as addled as a lightning struck hen. Examining him up close, I put his age at no more than fifteen or sixteen. Before I had a chance to start feeling sorry for him, I noticed he had a scalp tied to his rifle. It looked like a child's scalp. I jerked his tomahawk from his hand and swung it as hard as I could. He dropped like a rock.

Young he might have been but he was indeed one of the *'merciless Indian Savages, whose known rule of warfare, is an undistinguished destruction of all ages, sexes and conditions,'* that the Declaration of Independence referred to.

While I was getting my breath, Jacob and three militiamen caught up with me. Jacob looked at the carnage and asked, "Do you intend to win this war all by yourself or are you going to let General Washington help a little bit?"

"I guess I'll let him help. A little bit anyway."

"Good, I was afraid you might leave him out of it altogether."

"No, he can help."

"Are you sure?"

"Yeah, I'm sure."

"So, what were you doing out here alone."

I shrugged, "A man has to be somewhere doing something."

We gathered up the fallen Indians' weapons and gear. Like

Jacob said, a man could never have too much in the way of weapons and gear. I followed Jacob as he led the way back to the fort.

As we neared the gate, I said to Jacob, "Thanks for not chewing me out for being stupid."

"Hugh, I don't think I did you any favors. When Sarah gets through with you, you might wish one of those varmints had got you."

Jacob was right. Sarah was with the crowd that was waiting at the fort gate. When she saw all the blood on me, she paled and came over to me.

"You're hurt."

"Not bad, it's not my blood."

"It's not your blood?"

"It's not my blood."

"Good!"

With that comment, Sarah swung and hit me in the gut with her fist. Caught by surprise, I was nearly knocked down. It took me a minute to find my breath and ask, "What was that for?"

"That was for almost making me a widow before I was even a wife. That was for not coming to see me when you got to the fort the first time. That was for being a typical stupid man."

I looked to Jacob for help and real quick saw there would be no help from him. A glance at the others let me know that I was on my own. I started to try to explain why I had headed off into the forest but knew as I started that no explaining I could do would help anything. I also figured that this was not the time to tell her that we couldn't be married because she was rich and that I was not. I couldn't think of anything to say so I took her into my arms and kissed her.

I kissed her.

Now I hadn't meant to kiss her. I hadn't planned to kiss her. Both of us were a little stunned when I did. But I did and we did and neither one of us wanted to turn loose.

12

George Rogers Clark

Bowman's men brought the scalped body of Martin Kerry to Logan's Fort. He had got separated, or escaped, from Bowman's men when they turned to go to Fort Harrod. They found his body where I had fought with the Chickamauga. Another loyalist scalp for the King's agents to buy.

The tragic irony was that Martin Kerry's father was the King's agent who provided money for the scalps. Like Jacob said, he probably wouldn't appreciate the irony but when you unleash hellhounds, you can't always control who they bite.

Jacob straightened me out on a few things too. He said he had been bragging about me to Sarah through letters ever since we had partnered up. She had begun to become interested in me from reading her father's letters.

When Bowman returned to Logan's Fort, he brought a letter from George Rogers Clark for Jacob. Jacob read the letter, hesitated and put it in his pouch.

"Hugh, let's go see Sarah."

We found Sarah cooking a large kettle of stew for the fort. She tried not to show that she was glad to see me but the way she brightened up, I could tell that she was glad. I took the long wooden paddle from her and began to stir the stew.

"Do you think you know how to stir stew better than I do?"

"Oh no, not at all, I just needed something to do with my hands."

"So you just needed to do something with your hands and you think it's okay just to grab the stir paddle out of my hands and start stirring?"

"I thought as long as my hands were busy it'd be easier to resist grabbing you."

"Maybe you shouldn't resist so hard. If I don't want to be grabbed, I can let you know in a hurry."

Sarah placed a hand on each of her hips and turned to face her father. "Pa did you have a reason for coming to me besides bringing this betrothed of mine to pester me?"

"I come to protect him in case you decided to attack him again."

"And?"

"And to tell you that I have to go to Fort Harrod to meet with Clark."

"Clark?"

"George Rogers Clark."

"So you're going to take my betrothed away from me to go running off to Fort Harrod and the Lord knows where."

"I wasn't aiming to take Hugh along."

"Yes you are. I'm not aiming to have him underfoot, yanking a stirring paddle out of my hands any time he feels like it or grabbing me and kissing me any time he feels like it."

Sarah ladled stew into two tin cups and handed one to each of us.

"Now eat something before you start your trip and hurry back before I come to my senses and decide you're neither one worth taking care of."

We left after eating and arrived at Fort Harrod the next morning. It was my first time at Fort Harrod and I could see that it was larger than Logan's Fort and had more people. One of the first people we ran into was a rugged looking man, Jim Harrod. Jim had started the fort and settlement while Boone was still blazing his trace.

Jim was a noted and successful frontiersman. While widely regarded as uneducated, he kept his own records and had books in his cabin that he read. He had volunteered for service in the French and Indian war, right after his father died, when he was no more than ten or eleven years old. Of course he lied about his age to be sworn in to the militia but he had a good reputation of honesty. He had served under John Forbes in the French and Indian War and under Bouquet during the Pontiac Rebellion. After the Pontiac Rebellion, he traded and trapped the area north of the Ohio and east of the Mississippi Rivers. Living among French Traders, he picked up enough of the French language to communicate with the French. In addition to the French language, he learned several Indian languages and dialects.

In 1774, Jim was sent by the royal governor of Virginia, Lord Dunmore, to survey the bounds of land promised by the British government to soldiers who had fought in the French and Indian War. Jim and 37 men boated down the Monongahela and Ohio Rivers to the mouth of the Kentucky River. In June of 1774, almost a year before the treaty of Sycamore Shoals was completed, Jim and his men began the first white settlement in Kentucky. The settlement was called Harrod's Town. The thirty-eight men divided the land amongst them.

Harrod and his men had just finished the settlement's first log buildings when Daniel Boone and Michael Stoner reached them with news from Lord Dunmore that the Shawnee were now at war with Virginia. Harrod volunteered for duty and, as soon as the fighting was over, returned to Harrod's Town in Kentucky. The arrival of new settlers created the need for a larger fort, which was built. The settlers at Harrod's Town joined pioneers at Boonesborough to pass the first laws needed to govern what Richard Henderson called Transylvania. Harrod called it Kentucky and successfully opposed Henderson's Transylvania scheme. When Virginia created Kentucky County on December 31, 1776, Harrod's Town was made the county seat. Just recently Jim had become a justice in Kentucky County.

Jim filled us in on their recent Indian troubles, some of which we had already heard about. Jim concluded saying, "Jacob, somebody just this morning said 1777 was the year of the terrible sevens."

Jacob nodded and shifted his stance just a bit before he answered.

"Jim, I've been calling it the year of bloody sevens."

"Well, whether it's terrible or bloody, I'll be glad to see it past." Turning to me, Jim asked, "Is this old man hard to keep up with?"

"I shrugged and answered, "A man has to be somewhere doing something."

"That's for sure."

As we stepped away from Jim Harrod, I noticed a young man walking toward us who appeared to be just a few years older than I was. Jacob introduced him as George Rogers Clark. I had expected him to be older.

Jacob had filled me in on Clark a little bit. Clark left his home when he was nineteen to survey land in western Virginia. The following year, he entered Kentucky by coming down the Ohio River from Fort Pitt. Hundreds of settlers were taking advantage of the Treaty of Fort Stannic in 1768 to claim land in western Virginia and the Ohio River Valley. Just before the start of Lord Dunmore's War in 1774, Clark was gathering an expedition of almost one hundred men to lead down the Ohio River. His plans were changed when war broke out between Lord Dunmore and the Shawnee. The Shawnee tried to push the whites back but lost the major battle at Point Pleasant. Clark was made a captain in the Virginia Militia and served throughout the brief war. Clark did not believe Judge Richard Henderson's purchase of Kentucky at the Treaty of Sycamore Shoals or his idea of setting up a proprietary colony, to be called Transylvania, was legal. Like Ben Logan, Jim Harrod, and other settlers in Kentucky, George Rogers Clark didn't believe Transylvania had authority over them. In June of the previous year, settlers selected Clark and John Gabriel Jones to petition to the Virginia General Assembly to extend its boundary to include Kentucky. Clark and Jones traveled east over Skaggs Trace to the Hazel Patch and south on the Boone Trace, through Cumberland Gap and to Martin's Station. They found plenty of Indian sign and

Martin's Station abandoned. Fortunately, they were joined by other white men. They continued on to Williamsburg where they convinced Virginia Governor Patrick Henry to create Kentucky County as part of Virginia. Clark was also given 500 pounds of gunpowder and was made a major in the Virginia militia. As I already mentioned, Clark was not yet twenty-five years old but older settlers such as Boone and Logan, thought him a leader.

I could tell that Clark was chock full of confidence. He gripped my right hand and turned to Jacob.

"Jacob, have you got any letters lately?"

"Not since I picked some up that were waiting at Martin's Station. In July, I guess it was."

"Did you have anything that would shed any light on our Indian trouble?"

"There is speculation that in addition to hiring the German mercenaries that the British are paying Indians for scalps and captives."

"Does your information say this trouble is coming out of Detroit?"

"It does."

Clark hesitated and glanced at me. I figured he would be more comfortable if I were a little farther away and started to leave.

Jacob's voice stopped me, "Hugh!"

I stopped.

"Clark, anything you can't say to Hugh, don't say to me because I trust him with everything."

"Everything?"

"Everything including the ability to keep his mouth shut when he needs to. He's going to marry my daughter."

"Well, congratulations. Congratulations to both of you. Let's find a private place to talk."

What Clark wanted from Jacob was help with a proposal he was taking back to Williamsburg, Virginia. I listened and learned there was a Jacob that I had never seen before. This Jacob helped Clark form the arguments he would use to persuade the politicians in Williamsburg that an expedition to the Illinois country would help the Kentucky settlements.

We later learned that Clark was successful in persuading the politicians in Williamsburg and in securing the Northwest, capturing Hair Buyer Hamilton as a bonus. [12]

---

[12] *Clark came to believe that the only way to halt Indian raids into Kentucky was to attack British forts north of the Ohio River. He persuaded Virginia governor Patrick Henry to allow him to lead a force against enemy posts in the Illinois Country. Henry gave Clark the go-ahead and promoted him to the rank of lieutenant colonel. Clark was authorized to raise a force for the undertaking.*

Clark left Fort Pitt with 175 men in 1778. They canoed down the Ohio and captured Fort Massac at the mouth of the Tennessee River. Clark then proceeded overland to capture Kaskaskia without firing a shot on July 4. With cooperation from the French in Kaskaskia, who he had won over, Clark captured Cahokia five days later. A detachment was sent with a French Priest to take Vincennes on the Wabash River. Hearing of Clark's progress, the Hair Buyer Hamilton left Fort Detroit with over 500 men to attack the Americans. Vincennes, which was occupied by three militiamen, was easily taken. Hamilton released many of his men and settled in with a garrison of less than 100 men, intending that others would rejoin him when campaign weather came in the spring. Clark heard of the fort's recapture and made a winter march through freezing and flooded rivers to recapture the fort and make Hair Buyer Hamilton his prisoner.

13

HOME

We returned to Logan's Fort two days later. Jacob seemed calm enough to anyone who was paying any attention but I knew his head was buzzing with what we had learned. I knew that my head was buzzing. One thing that I knew was that George Rogers Clark was going to be a leader unless he was killed or taken down by jealous men who weren't fit to sharpen his knife.

Jacob explained, "A lot of men are ambitious but fewer men have the courage and ability to achieve their ambition. George Rogers Clark is the whole thing. He has ambition, character, courage, good sense, ability. As long as lesser men are afraid to tackle what he tackles, he will succeed. When lesser men figure that most of the danger is gone, they will blame him for doing something, anything where they would have dared to do nothing. They will question his deeds and actions with the safety of hindsight and distance. He is who Kentucky needs, He's who this country needs but weaker, jealous men will damage his reputation."

"Jacob, I'd follow him to Hell before breakfast."

"I would too, Hugh. I wish I didn't know what I was talking about."

I hoped that Jacob was wrong but I had never known Jacob to be wrong when talking about people. I don't know how he did it but Jacob knew a sight more about how people acted and what made them act that way than anyone else I knew.[13]

As we entered the fort gates, I thought I saw Sarah brighten. If she did, it didn't last because as we reached her she frowned and handed me a wooden water bucket.

"Don't think you can come in here empty handed with me needing water.

She then picked up a second bucket. I reached for the second bucket and she nearly bit my head off.

"You can't carry two buckets and your gun too. Pick up your gun so that you can protect me."

We walked to the spring. There were two militiamen between the forest and spring. As we got further from the fort, Sarah seemed to get a spring in her step. Her arms swung a little livelier. She was smiling. There was no sign of the sharp-tongued girl who handed me the water bucket. I started to point out that she would have been guarded by the two militiamen without me when she dropped her bucket and pulled me into the shade by spring. While I looked around to see if I had missed some danger that she had seen, she hugged me tightly.

"Hugh, I missed you."

---

[13] Jacob was right. George Rogers Clark accomplished a great deal for Kentucky, Virginia and the United States. He did all this between the ages of 24 and 30. As the frontier grew safer, rumors about Clark began to be whispered, his decisions and actions questioned and the receipts he turned in to receive payment for those who helped and supplied him vanished for over 100 years.

"Sometimes you got a strange way of showing it."

"It's nobody's concern how we feel about each other but ours. I am not going to allow anyone else to know how much I feel about you."

"I don't understand. You've barely seen me."

"My father has written about you ever since you began working with him. He is very pleased with you. He says you will take over his letter writing. Just reading about you in my father's letters caused me to be impressed by you. I think that is when I began to fall in love with you."

"Well, a man has to be somewhere doing something."

Sarah stood on her toes and pulled my face down. She kissed my lips and whispered, "I knew you would say that."

November 1777

Jacob and I rode into Raleigh, North Carolina on a chilly and rainy November day. The news of Burgoyne's surrender at Saratoga was still new enough for people to celebrate and be excited about.

Jacob had spent much of the trip east teaching me how to make money work for me. Some of his rules were:

- If you need it, get the best you can afford
- If you don't need it and can't make money from it, don't get it
- If you can't afford it, don't get it
- To borrow is to indenture yourself
- Never lend without collateral

- It is better to invest in than to lend to

Jacob and I left our horses at a stable and arranged for their care and feed. Jacob then led me to a bank where I listened while he went over his accounts. The banker seemed a little uncomfortable at my presence until Jacob told him, "Hugh is my son-in-law. You can talk in his presence."

Now I wasn't sure that I was really his son in law. Sarah and I had been married by Ben Logan. She had insisted that it would do until we could be married by a 'real preacher.' She seemed happy with the arrangement and if she was happy then I was overjoyed.

In fact, I had never been so happy.

After the banking business was completed, Jacob asked, "What can you tell me about a banker name of Kerry?"

"I don't really know the man. I can't really discuss him."

"If you like my business you will and you won't hold back anything."

"Well, in that case, he is thought to be a loyalist."

"Go on."

"He seems to be wealthy."

"Does he seem to be wealthier than his banking business warrants?"

Reluctantly, the banker nodded, "Yes."

"Do you have any idea where he gets his wealth from?"

"Uh, no."

"Is he involved in any business?"

"He is a partner in a business that trades with the Indians."

"And what is the story on a lawyer named Felton?"

"He is hand in glove with Kerry."

"So both Felton and Kerry are Tories?"

"I think so. They don't air their views but I think so."

"You know how this town works. Where can I find an honest lawyer?"

"Our Lawyer, Matthew Blevins." After a moment he added, "I'll send for him."

Jacob rose and nodded. "We are going to the Sir Walter Raleigh Tavern. What I have to say shouldn't be said by a man completely sober. Send Matthew Blevins to us."

The Sir Walter Raleigh Tavern was a large two floored building. The first floor was divided into a kitchen and storage area, the owners living quarters, an area that focused on serving drinks and a room with a single, long dining table. It was built of bricks and was framed by huge fireplaces at each end of the building. The upper floor held several rooms for sleeping and a large common room for travelers who either couldn't afford the cost of a single room or didn't feel the need for a single room. Travelers could also rent sleeping space on the floors of the dining room and the drinking area.

It was an hour before Blevins met us at the Tavern. We had each had a hot rum toddy to ease the chill followed by a tankard of ale.

I noticed a moderately well-dressed man approaching.   He stopped at our table and said, "Hello Jacob."

"Hello Matthew."

That caught me a little by surprise because I had no idea that they already knew each other.   I sat up to listen and keep my mouth shut.

"Jacob, your letters have been interesting and informative."

"As have yours."

Jacob gestured to a chair and Matthew sat down.   Jacob carefully told Matthew what we had learned from Martin Kerry's drunk companions.

Matthew listened carefully and asked, "How do you want to do this Jacob?"

"Confront Felton and Kerry in front of witnesses."

"They should both be in here within the hour."

"Can you round up some friendly witnesses and assistance?"

"Yes."

Half an hour later, several local militia leaders were seated in the tavern. Ten minutes later, two middle aged men walked in together. They were roughly Jacob's age but nowhere near as fit. Matthew nodded to Jacob.

I had no idea what Jacob was going to do. We were still dressed in the buckskin clothing we had left Logan's fort wearing. We each carried our knife and tomahawk. We were unshaven and needed a wash. Jacob walked up to where the two sat and said, "Kerry, I understand you trade with the Chickamauga."

Kerry and Felton looked up at Jacob, then looked at each other. Felton motioned and two rough looking men came from opposite sides of the tavern. I stepped forward and grabbed one's hair from behind and jerked him back. He hit the floor hard and stayed still when he saw the knife in my hand. A Militia officer and two of his men herded the second man back to a bench.

Felton stood and asked, "Were you addressing me?"

"You and Kerry."

"If you have business with us, you can come by my office tomorrow."

"First, I want to know one thing. How much did Kerry pay for his son, Martin Kerry's scalp?"

Kerry jumped up. "What are you talking about?"

"When your son brought Chickamauga to Kentucky to steal my daughter and kill me, he got separated and lost. He was ambushed and killed by Indians, probably Chickamauga. They scalped him."

Jacob waited for Kerry to respond but Kerry just shook his head.

"Kerry, the three men with your son told us everything. Felton has a letter with an inheritance for my daughter Sarah. Your plan was for your son to take Chickamauga to Kentucky to kill me and steal Sarah. Your son Martin Kerry was then going to fake a rescue in an attempt to marry her."

Felton was looking for a way to leave but quickly saw there was none. Kerry looked dazed and continued shaking his head.

"Kerry, I know that you have been supplying the Chickamauga for the British."

Kerry didn't reply except to shake his head.

Jacob took a deep breath and roared, **"HOW MUCH DID YOUR SON'S SCALP COST THE KING?   HOW MUCH DID YOUR SON'S SCALP COST YOU?"**

Kerry broke down. He was taken back to his office by three militiamen to produce his list of contacts and the people who supplied him. Jacob twisted Felton's arm behind his back had walked him behind Kerry.

"Felton, if there is evidence you stole a shilling from my daughter, I'll give your scalp to the Indians."

Two days later, Jacob's business was completed and we were both on our way back to Logan's Fort and Kentucky. Jacob noticed me grinning and asked, "Hugh, what's so funny?"

"I was just wondering what Sarah was going to find to complain about when we get home."

It wouldn't matter. I was going home.

EPILOUGUE

JACOB'S CONCLUSIONS AS DERIVED FROM NUMOUROUS LETTERS RECEIVED FROM ALL PARTS OF THE UNITED STATES REGARDING BRITISH ACTIONS IN 1777

Written in 1795

The British should have had the war won.

George Washington and the Continental Congress made a mistake in trying to hold New York with an untrained army and no navy. The British Navy gave mobility to the British army and loyalists gave information to the British'. It was not any miracle that the British captured New York. It was either a miracle or the help of The Almighty that Washington and his army escaped.

After capturing New York, The British should have had the war won.

Washington escaped with an army but by anybody's reckoning, he was whipped. Short on supplies, short on enthusiasm and soon to be short on men as the enlistments of most of his soldiers were about to expire. Washington commanded an army that was cold, hungry and demoralized. The only luck that the United States and General Washington had, other than escaping from New York, was the capture of General Charles Lee by the British.

Despite laudatory credentials, I do not believe General Charles Lee was any assistance to General Washington.

Still, the British should have had the war won.

Despite, or perhaps because of the difficulties he faced. Washington resolved to attack the Hessians at Trenton New Jersey on the day after their Christmas celebrations. Moving soldiers and artillery across the ice choked Delaware River and marching them in bitter cold to Trenton was a feat that Americans should long celebrate.

Many of the Continentals wrapped rags around their feet and some had no shoes. Boats manned by Colonel John Glover's Regiment of fishermen from Marblehead, Massachusetts ferried men and artillery across the ice filled river. Over 2500 Continentals crossed the Delaware River between twilight, and 4:00 in the morning. Two miles later Washington separated his army into two columns. General Greene, with a division of around 1,200 men and ten cannons, accompanied General Washington. General Sullivan's division of around 1,300 men marched down the River Road. When Washington received a courier from Sullivan telling him that the storm was making muskets unfit for firing, Washington responded by ordering the courier to tell Sullivan to use the bayonet, that he was resolved to take Trenton.

Arriving later than anticipated, Washington's Army surprised a Hessian picket a half mile outside Trenton. Despite their resistance, the Hessians were quickly captured or forced into retreating. While this skirmish was happening, General Sullivan and his Continentals reached Trenton and fired their cannon at the Hessian barracks. Washington advanced his Continentals as the Hessians tried to sober up enough to form a resistance. The Continentals placed six cannon in a commanding position at the juncture of two main thoroughfares. The Continentals rushed into positions to take control of the Princeton road to prevent any Hessians escaping. Continentals from General Sullivan's division drove Hessians from their positions and seized the Bordentown road bridge. The Hessians tried to form a resistance. Hessian artillery tried to fire two cannons. Before they could fire, they were overwhelmed and captured by Continental troops led by Captain William Washington, a kinsman of General Washington. The Hessian Commander, Colonel Rall, tried to counter attack with his Hessians but they instead retreated to an orchard where Rall was shot from his horse.

General Washington and his ragged Continentals won a resounding, one sided, victory. The town of Trenton was defended by a force of over 1,500 trained and battle hardened Hessians commanded by veteran officers. The American Continentals completely surprised the Hessians who were not able to mount a defense. The Hessian commander was killed. The Hessians surrendered after losing 150 killed or wounded. Over nine hundred Hessians were made prisoners and 500 Hessians escaped.

Suddenly, it was a brand new war.

On January 2, 1777 General Cornwallis marched on Trenton with six thousand men. The Americans began a fighting withdrawal. American soldiers ambushed Cornwallis' soldiers on the march, causing delays while the British sent out flanking parties. The British reached Trenton around four P.M. to find Washington entrenched but he was both heavily outnumbered and outclassed. Washington had around five thousand men but many of them were militia who were both untried and untrained.

Washington deployed his troops to on the south side of the Assunpink Creek. From that strong position he repelled several attempts by the British to capture the bridge. Night fell and Cornwallis decided to wait to attack at dawn. By some accounts, his officers wanted to attack right away due to Washington's known ability to retreat and escape.

Washington left a few men to keep campfires burning and make entrenchment noises. With the rest of his army, he went around the British forces and marched his army toward Princeton. Washington's goal was to attack the rear of the British forces and capture a 70,000 pound sterling war chest of General Howe in New Brunswick. Washington led his men in silence over back roads to the south and around the British. Washington's army then marched toward Princeton. Providence or The Almighty helped America again by freezing the muddy roads making them passable for both men and cannon.

At dawn, British Colonel Mawhood (who had been held in reserve) placed his forces in motion and marched to assist Cornwallis. General Mercer and his Continentals were guarding Washington's left flank. Mawhood and Mercer stumbled on each other and formed to attack. Mercer and Mawhood each thought they had come up against a patrol. Mawhood has almost 300 men, and Mercer roughly 100 men with 200 following. Both sides rushed to form a battle line on high ground. Mercer found Mawhood's men already deployed in line. After exchanging volleys, the British charged with bayonets. Mercers men fell back as fewer than two dozen have bayonets and most are armed with rifles which took longer to reload. Mercer was mortally wounded. His troops fell back until reinforced by Cadwalader's 600 Pennsylvania militiamen.

Maintaining good order, they fired and fell back. Washington and his officers arrived to rally them. When more Continentals joined him, Washington led them against the British Line. When only 30 yards from the British, Washington ordered his Continentals and militia to fire. Both sides fired volleys. Astonishingly Mawhood's British regulars broke and ran. Washington immediately ordered a charge. The British troops retreated while Washington personally led the chase.

The British 40th and 55th regiments were set up in defensive positions and prepared to defend Princeton. General Sullivan swept into Princeton from the other end, The British sent a force to attempt to outflank them. Sullivan responded by sending a stronger force to counter the British flanking maneuver and forced the British back. Sullivan met a large number of British deployed behind a dike. Sullivan didn't hesitate. Sullivan deployed his cannon which shot into the dike, driving the British into the main college building. The Americans fired two cannon shots into the building and the British inside wisely surrendered.

Like I said, suddenly, it was a brand new war. The Continental army had showed the British it could stand and fight.

Washington broke off the chase of the fleeing British when they were reinforced. He shifted his force to keep them from being flanked by Cornwallis and withdrew to a better defensive position. He decided that his tired soldiers had done all they could do for the time being. Even as Cornwallis arrived and drew his army into a battle line, Washington and his army escaped. He moved his Army into winter quarters at Morristown, New Jersey.

Following the American victories at Trenton and Princeton, the British Commander ordered New Jersey to be abandoned with the exception of a line between New Brunswick and Perth Amboy.

Suddenly, it was a brand new war.

Suddenly, the British had problems that they had not

foreseen. Based on all the letters that I have received (over 100), I believe that the British at this time decided to sic the Indians on the American Frontier. IN April 1777, the Mohawk leader, Joseph Brant, began to recruit men to fight for the British. Over half these men were white Tories who had been forced to flee when the British couldn't protect them.

I have been told that Brant's sister was a wife or consort of Sir William Johnson. In June, he held a meeting with William Johnson and William's son. Johnson provisioned Brant's party under the promise that Colonel John Butler would pay for them. That same month, a British army, led by General John Burgoyne marched south from Canada in an attempt to split the New England states from the rest of the United States. Burgoyne had an army of nearly eight thousand British and Hessian soldiers and nearly one thousand Indians.

It was also in June 1777 that letters began appearing along the Kentucky frontier, sometimes on the mutilated bodies of settlers, stating that those who swore allegiance to King George III and England would not be harmed and would receive free land.

Of course, attacks on the Kentucky frontier began in March and the danger continued until winter weather set in. My suspicion has always been that the attacks were paid for by the British and many or most would not have occurred without British financial backing and provocation.

The Tory colonel, John Butler, was ordered from Fort Niagara by the governor of Canada to join an expedition through the Mohawk Valley being led by St. Leger. A large number of Indians accompanied St. Leger.

The British planned to split New England from the rest of the American colonies. Burgoyne was to strike from Canada by way of the Champlain Valley to Albany, capturing Fort Ticonderoga while in rout. St. Leger was to sail down Lake Ontario to Oswego then move down the Mohawk Valley, capture Fort Stanwix and rendezvous with Burgoyne at Albany. General Howe, was to move north from New York and rendezvous with Burgoyne at Albany.

The British plan started to work. Burgoyne forced General St. Clair to abandon Fort Ticonderoga. St. Clair's army escaped and laid barriers across the roads and trails to slow Burgoyne. Colonel Hale and Colonel Francis deployed their men as a rear guard for the retreating Continentals. This rear guard was attacked by British General Fraser and the Hessian Colonel Baron Von Riedesel. In an intense battle, the Continentals were forced to retreat.

St. Leger paid a bunch of Indians to join his attack on Fort Stanwix. Indians then attacked three girls picking raspberries close to the fort, killing and scalping two and wounding the third. St. Leger sent a demand to the fort that the Americans surrender. Fort Stanwix refused the demand. St. Leger threatened to unleash his Indians if the fort did not surrender. He then began a siege of the fort.

General Nicholas Herkimer ordered the militia to assemble. The following day, approximately 800 militiamen began their march to Fort Schuyler. They were ambushed near the Oneida Indian village of Oriska in what is now called the battle of Oriskany. Both sides were evenly matched and both sides lost heavily.

The British and Indians lost more than they gained. Members of the Iroquois Six Nations were on both sides of the battle and both lost men.

During the battle of Oriskany, militiamen raided the unguarded camps of St Leger and his Indian allies, carrying away everything they could. This served to discourage the Indians further in that not only did they lose too many men but they lost property as well.

Benedict Arnold then led a relief mission that forced St. Leger to retreat.

General Burgoyne received a report that settlers in the Connecticut River Valley had hundreds of horses that could be confiscated. The report failed to mention that General John Stark, a friend and correspondent from my service with Rogers Rangers in the French and Indian War, was at Bennington with a sizeable number of men. Burgoyne ordered the Hessian Colonel Friedrich Baum to lead a force of roughly eight hundred men and confiscate the horses. Stark attacked Baum and defeated him, killing over two hundred and making prisoners of the rest.

On one hand, Washington wasn't having much luck. He lost the Battle of Brandywine due to faulty information but was able to withdraw his army. Hearing of the defeat, the Continental Congress fled Philadelphia to York Pennsylvania. Days later, General "Mad" Anthony Wayne's were attacked at night and he lost over one hundred men, but saved his cannon and most of his men. The British army captured and occupied Philadelphia.

Fortunately for the United States and for Kentuckians, General "Mad" Anthony Wayne learned from his experiences and was later called "the man who cannot be surprised" by some of the Indians in Ohio.

Despite General Horatio Gates being placed in command of the forces opposing Burgoyne, The Americans won their first encounter, known as the First Battle of Saratoga. Despite Gates and most reports say thanks to Benedict Arnold, Burgoyne was defeated at the second battle and being unable to retreat, was forced to surrender.

Ironically, Burgoyne's use of Indians helped lead to his defeat. Volunteers flocked to Gates after learning of the murder and scalping of Jane McCrea. Jane McCrea was affianced to a loyalist militia officer, Jane traveled with her aunt to join her fiancé. She stopped to stay at the home of loyalists in the village of Fort Edwards. The village was attacked by Burgoyne's Indians who killed and massacred residents and captured Jane and her aunt.

Two Indians argued over ownership of Jane. One then killed and scalped her. The band of Indians then returned to Burgoyne, celebrating their "victory" with loud shouting and boasting. Jane's fiancé, seeing her aunt and the scalp of Jane immediately recognized both. His outcry of the crime demonstrated Burgoyne's total lack of control of his Indian mercenaries. Not only could he not control them, neither could he punish them.

I have noted that two of the three columns of assault, Burgoyne's and St. Leger's, depended on Indian support and the fear that such support would engender. In this, the British completely misread the American character. Rather than being cowed into submission, the Americans attacked the threat. I do not think the British will ever understand that aspect of the American character.

The massacre of loyalists was publicized by patriots and used to arouse the people. Loyalists began to realize that unless they were actually in the presence of the British army, that they had no protection from the British paid Indians. Some loyalists fled to the protection of the British Army in New York, which meant they were not growing food to sell to the British army. Other loyalists began to rethink their allegiances and some switched sides. The news of loyalist deaths by Indians increased the bad feelings toward the British and was used as an effective recruiting tool. Volunteers and militia flocked to help defeat Burgoyne at Saratoga.

Outside of Philadelphia, Washington wasn't giving up or conceding anything. In early October, he led his force of 8,000 Continentals and roughly 2500 militia against over 9,000 British regulars at Germantown, Pennsylvania. A heavy fog rolled in causing much confusion. Some Continental units fired on each other. Washington was forced to order a withdrawal. Despite having to withdraw, the Continentals once again proved they could stand and hold their own against the British.

Between the successes of the battles of Saratoga and

Washington's army attacking the British at Germantown (even though conditions forced them to withdraw), the French openly allied with us, America. Victory was still a few years away.

Yes, victory was still a few years away but I knew it was coming. Sometimes I think it is good that victory did not come easily and that the war lasted long enough to expose character flaws in some of our leaders. Generals Charles Lee and Horatio Gates specifically.

With all that was happening east of the mountains, the Continental congress was not able to send much in the way of assistance to those of us who were struggling west of the mountains in Kentucky. Fortunately, the state of Virginia was able to provide Colonel Bowman and his men along with some powder and lead.

The year of bloody sevens ended with General and his army settling into winter quarters at a place called Valley Forge.

We in Kentucky hunkered down, kept our powder dry and prepared for the worst. We figured two things; one, we knew could handle the worst, and we also knew the worst wouldn't last forever. By hiring the Indians to attack us, paying them for both scalps and captives, the British condemned the Indians. Few if any settlers who lost a friend or family member to the savagery of the Shawnee and other tribes will ever have sympathy for their plight or circumstances. Daniel Boone is said to be very understanding about them but I know that his brother Squire is not and I have some doubts about how Daniel feels about the Indians. Still, Daniel Boone was raised a Quaker and the teaching might have stuck with him better than it did with Squire Boone.

Indian attacks on Kentucky settlers and settlements still continued, even though the war for American independence ended for all intents and purposes when Cornwallis surrendered his army at Yorktown in October 1781. This surrender was four years after Burgoyne surrendered at Saratoga. British led attacks continued in

Kentucky after 1777. British and Indians came again against Boonesborough in 1778. They also attacked with cannon, and took Ruddell's Station and Martin's Station in 1780. Indians attacked the surrendered settlers after Ruddell surrendered, killing men, women and children. The last British led attack in Kentucky was the attack on Bryan's Station in August 1782 and was followed by the ambush at the Blue Licks. It should be noted that our defeat at the battle of Blue Licks in August, 1982 occurred ten months after Cornwallis surrendered. I have always suspected that the British goal was to confine the United States to a strip between the Atlantic Ocean and the Appalachian Mountains. They did not succeed in chasing us out of Kentucky, however.

I can't help wondering what or how present and future relationships between the red men and white men would have been if the British hadn't paid them as mercenaries. Few people on the frontier who have buried the mutilated remains of tortured kin and friends have any trust or compassion for the Indians who sided with the British for pay. This distrust and hate may last for generations.

Kentucky became a state three years ago in 1792. Kentucky is the fifteenth state in our United States. I am proud to say I had a hand in that. Like Hugh says. "A man has to be some-where doing something."

I am very pleased to say that our Indian troubles may be over. My statement may be a little premature but the Ohio Indians to the north and the Chickamauga to the south were both defeated a year ago, in August 1794.

My old friend Billy Whitley finally struck a solid blow at the Chickamauga. Billy, now a colonel of the 6th Regiment of Kentucky militia, with Col. Montgomery of the Tennessee militia served with Major James Ore who was designated to command the expedition by Tennessee Governor Blount. They focused their attention on two Chickamauga villages, Nickajack and Running Water, as their targets. These villages had been identified as the source of numerous raiding parties. The army reached Nickajack in August and found it deserted except for roughly a hundred warriors. Most of the Chickamauga fled to Running Water before the army arrived. Warriors from Running Water were coming to reinforce Nickajack. They met the fleeing Chickamauga and all the warriors returned to Nickajack. They arrived after the battle had begun and the Chickamauga warriors were already in retreat. The arriving reinforcements met the retreating warriors and they tried to make a stand against the white army. It was a complete disaster for the Chickamauga. They were routed with many losses and only wounded three whites. Both Villages were destroyed and almost one hundred Chickamauga were killed. Whitley personally shot a warrior out of a moving canoe at a far distance after his men had failed hit the warrior.

Also in August 1794 General Anthony Wayne and his army defeated Little Turtle and his Shawnee ally, Blue Jacket, not far from the British illegal outpost of Fort Miami. General Wayne spent two years training and disciplining his army. In June, Wayne's army repelled an Indian attack on Fort Recovery. This was the place where General St. Clair's army was defeated three years earlier. In August, General Wayne out thought his enemy. They waited for his attack and fasted until he actually attacked. By the time he attacked, the Indians were tired and hungry. Two thousand Indians attacked Wayne's nine hundred soldiers. Blue Jacket tried to use trees knocked down by a tornado as cover but within a few hours Wayne's soldiers rallied and drove Blue Jacket and his warriors from the protection of the fallen timber. The soldiers chased the Indians to the gate of the British Fort. The British did not allow Indians to enter the fort, which forced them to flee. Wayne's army killed over 200 Indians and shamed the British by revealing the British could not help the Indians fight the Americans. Hugh was there as were a good many other good Kentuckians.

Hugh and Sarah were married by the first circuit riding preacher that came to Logan's Fort. Now, many years later, they have given me seven grandchildren and lots of joy. Hugh helps me with my *letter writing and is developing into the man I always knew he would become.*

The one regret I have is the way the United States and Virginia, and I guess Kentucky too, have treated George Rogers Clark. He did more to save Kentucky and the Northwest than any other man that I can think of right now. He led by force of his confidence and personality. The United States owes George Rogers Clark for the territory that is now Ohio, Indiana and Illinois. Right now, he can't own an acre of land without being sued for it nor can he earn a dollar without being sued for it. He lives in a cabin on his brother's land with only a jug to help him forget his country's ingratitude.

ABOUT THE AUTHOR

The author, Charles E. Hayes, MSgt, USAF (Ret.) spent 24 years in the United States Air Force. He is a former school teacher and an avid re-enactor. He currently helps other veterans through the auspices of the Disabled American Veterans in Kentucky.

Other Books by Charles E. Hayes

- Out of the Jungle
- The Sword of Gideon
- Listening to Night Winds at Blue Licks
- Ambush at the Blue Licks
- Gideon Strikes (due out December 2014)

Made in the USA
Middletown, DE
24 April 2023

29263736R00080